Out on Main Street

Kelly Langgard
Calgary, 1994

Out on Main Street

& OTHER STORIES

SHANI MOOTOO

PRESS GANG PUBLISHERS

VANCOUVER

93 94 95 96 97 5 4 3 2 1

"Lemon Scent" was originally published under the title "A Three-Part Story" in
The Skin on Our Tongues, a special issue of *absinthe* (Summer 1993).

The Publisher gratefully acknowledges financial assistance from the Canada
Council and the Cultural Services Branch, Province of British Columbia.

CANADIAN CATALOGUING IN PUBLICATION DATA

Mootoo, Shani, 1957 –
Out on Main Street and other stories
    ISBN 0-88974-052-6
    I. Title.
PS8576.065908 1993   C813'.54   C93-091774-X
PR9199.3.M65908 1993

Edited for the press by Ramabai Espinet
Design by Valerie Speidel
Cover illustration © 1993 by Kausar Nigita. From an original woodblock print.
Author photograph by Sara Bailey
Typeset in Adobe Caslon
Printed and bound in Canada by Best Gagné Book Manufacturers Inc.
Printed on acid-free paper

Press Gang Publishers
603 Powell Street
Vancouver, B.C. V6A 1H2
Canada

For my sisters,
Vahli and Indrani,
and my brothers,
Kavir and Romesh Jr.

and for my dear friend
Persimmon Blackbridge

Acknowledgements

In the summer of 1992, during the Race and The Body Politic residency at the Banff Centre for the Arts, I wrote "Out on Main Street" and "The Upside-downness of the World as it Unfolds." There I met several people who gave me invaluable feedback on these two stories (and ongoing friendship) – among them I would like to offer my sincerest thanks to Christine Almeida, Kerri Sakamoto, Shauna Beharry, Donna James and Chris Creighton-Kelly.

My good friends Aruna Srivastava, Larissa Lai, David Olsen, Cyndia Cole, Brenda McIntyre, Zool Suleman and Musa Janmohamed have been very indulgent, massaging my ego and holding me back from doubting.

I owe so very much to Persimmon Blackbridge and Shelina Velji for their unconditional friendships and unqualified trust in me. Appreciation for their kind support goes far beyond words.

Yasmin Ladha's critiques and feedback are thoroughly appreciated. Ramabai Espinet's knowledge and understanding of "back-home" were invaluable in the editing of this book. I am also very grateful for Robin Van Heck's excellent fine-tooth comb and Barbara Kuhne's eagle eye and generous persistence.

It has been an absolute pleasure to work with the Press Gang Publishing Collective – Barbara, Della and Val – creating friendship, adventure and pleasure out of business!

Regretfully, many names are omitted – not excluded, but omitted only because of space. I wish I could just go on and on…

Which of us, here, can possibly know the intimacies of each other's cupboards "back-home," or in which hard-to-reach corners dust-balls used to collect?
(Or didn't?)

One's interpretation of fact is another's fiction, and one's fiction is someone else's bafflement.

Contents

A Garden of Her Own

A north-facing balcony meant that no sunlight would enter there. A deep-in-the-heart-of-the-forest green pine tree, over-fertilized opulence extending its midriff, filled the view from the balcony.

There was no window, only a glass sliding door which might have let fresh air in and released second- or third-hand air and the kinds of odours that build phantoms in stuffy apartments. But it remained shut. Not locked, but stuck shut from decades of other renters' black, oily grit and grime which had collected in the grooves of the sliding door's frame.

Vijai knew that it would not budge up, down or sideways. For the amount of rent the husband paid for this bachelor apartment, the landlord could not be bothered. She opened the hallway door to let the cooking lamb fat and garlic smells drift out into the hallway. She did not want them to burrow into the bed sheets, into towels and clothes crammed into the dented cream-coloured metal space-saver cupboard that she had to share with the husband. It was what all the other renters did too; everyone's years of oil – sticky, burnt, over-used, rancid oil – and of garlic, onions and spices formed themselves into an impenetrable nose-singeing, skin-stinging presence that lurked menacingly in the hall. Instead of releasing the lamb from the husband's apartment, opening the door allowed this larger phantom to barge its way in.

Vijai, engulfed, slammed the door shut. She tilted her head to face the ceiling and breathed in hard, searching for air that had no smell, no weight. The husband was already an hour late for dinner. She paced the twelve strides, back and forth, from the balcony door to the hall door, glancing occasionally at the two table settings, stopping to straighten his knife, his fork, the napkin, the flowers, his knife, his fork, the napkin, the flowers. Her arms and legs tingled weakly and her intestines filled up with beads of acid formed out of unease and fear. Seeing a smear of her fingerprint on the husband's knife, she picked it up and polished it on her T-shirt until it gleamed brilliantly, and she saw in it her mother's eyes looking back at her.

*

Sunlight. I miss the sunlight – yellow light and a sky ceiling miles high. Here the sky sits on my head, heavy grey with snow and freezing rain. I miss being able to have doors and windows opened wide, never shut except sometimes in the rainy season. Rain, rain, pinging on, winging off the galvanized tin roof. But always warm rain. No matter how much it rained, it was always warm.

And what about the birds? Flying in through the windows how often? Two, three times a week? Sometimes even twice in a single day. In the shimmering heat you could see them flying slowly, their mouths wide open as if crying out soundlessly. They would actually be flicking their tongues at the still air, gulping and panting, looking for a window to enter and a curtain rod to land on to cool off. But once they had cooled off and were ready to fly off again, they could never seem to focus on the window to fly through and they would bang themselves against the walls and the light shade until they fell, panicked and stunned. I was the one who would get the broom and push it gently up toward one of these birds after it looked like it had cooled off, and prod, prod, prod until it hopped onto the broom and then I would lower it and reach from behind and cup the trembling in my hand. I can, right now, feel the life, the heat in the palm of my hand from the little body, and the fright in its tremble. I would want to hold on to it, even think of placing it in a cage and looking after it, but something always held me back. I would put my mouth close to its ears and whisper calming shh shh shhhhs, and then take it, pressed to my chest, out the back door and open my hand and wait for it to take its time fluffing out right there in my open hand before flying away.

But here? There are hardly any birds here, only that raucous, aggressive old crow that behaves as if it owns the scraggly pine tree it sits in across the street. This street is so noisy! Every day, all day and all night long, even on Sundays, cars whiz by, ambulances and fire trucks pass screaming, and I think to myself thank goodness it couldn't be going for anyone I know. I don't know anyone nearby.

Too much quiet here, too shut off. Not even the sound of children playing in the street, or the sound of neighbours talking to each other over fences, conversations floating in through open windows, open bricks. Here even when doors are open people walk down hallways with their noses straight ahead, making a point of not glancing to even nod hello.

Oh! This brings all kinds of images to my mind: the coconut tree outside my bedroom brushing, scraping, swishing against the wall. Green-blue iridescent lizards clinging, upside down, to the ceiling above my bed.

And dinner time. Mama's voice would find me wherever I was. "Vijai, go and tell Cheryl to put food on the table, yuh father comin home just now." Standing in one place, at the top of her meagre voice she would call us one by one: "Bindra, is dinner time. Bindra, why you so harden, boy? Dinner gettin cold. Turn off that TV right now! Shanti, come girl, leave what you doin and come and eat. Vashti, go and tell Papa dinner ready, and then you come and sit down." Sitting down, eating together. Talking together. Conversations with no boundaries, no false politeness, no need to impress Mama or Papa.

But that's not how it was always. Sometimes Papa didn't come home till long after suppertime. Mama would make us eat but she would wait for him. Sometimes he wouldn't come for days, and she would wait for him then too.

But there were always flowers from the garden on the table. Pink and yellow gerberas, ferns, ginger lilies. That was your happiness, eh Mama? the garden, eh? And when there were blossoms you and I would go outside together. You showed me how to angle the garden scissors so that the plant wouldn't hurt for too long. We would bring in the bundle of flowers and greenery with their fresh-cut garden smell and little flying bugs and spiders, and you would show me how to arrange them for a centrepiece or a corner table or a floor piece. The place would look so pretty! Thanks for showing that to me, Mama.

Mama, he's never brought me any flowers. Not even a dandelion.

I don't want him to ask how much these cost. Don't ask me who sent them. No one sent them; I bought them myself. With my own money. My own money.

He's never given me anything. Only money for groceries.

Late. Again.

I jabbed this lamb with a trillion little gashes and stuffed a clove of garlic in each one with your tongue, your taste buds in mind. I spent half the day cooking this meal and you will come late and eat it after the juices have hardened to a candle-wax finish, as if it were nothing but a microwave dinner.

I want a microwave oven.

Mama, why did you wait to eat? If I were to eat now would you, Papa, he think I am a bad wife? Why did you show me this, Mama?

I must not nag.

*

Vijai remained sleeping until the fan in the bathroom woke her. It sputtered raucously, like an airplane engine starting up, escalating in time to fine whizzing, lifting off into the distance.

Five-thirty, Saturday morning.

She had fretted through most of the night, twisting, arching her body, drawing her legs up to her chest, to the husband's chest, rolling, and nudging him, hoping that he would awaken to pull her body into his and hold her there. She wanted to feel the heat of his body along the length of hers, his arms pressing her to him. Or his palm placed flat on her lower belly, massaging, touching her. He responded to her fidgeting once and she moved closer to him to encourage him, but he turned his naked back to her and continued his guttural exhaling, inhaling, sounding exactly like her father.

Eventually Vijai's eyes, burning from salty tears that had spilled and dampened the pillow under her cheek, fluttered shut and she slept, deep and dreamless, until the fan awakened her.

When the sound of the shower water snapping at the enamel tub was muffled against his body, she pulled herself over to lie in and smell his indentation in the tired foam mattress. She inhaled, instead, the history of the mattress: unwashed hair, dying skin, old and rancid sweat – not the smell she wanted to nestle in. Neither would the indentation cradle her; she could feel the protruding shape of the box-spring beneath the foam.

She debated whether to get up and thanklessly make his toast and tea, or pretend not to have awakened, the potential for blame nagging at her. She slid back to her side of his bed, the other side of the line that he had drawn down the middle with the cutting edge of his outstretched hand. Vijai pulled her knees to her chest and hugged them. When the shower stopped she hastily straightened herself out and put her face inside the crack between the bed and the rough wall. Cold from the wall transferred itself onto her cheek, and layers upon layers of human smells trapped behind cream-coloured paint pierced her nostrils.

Vijai was aware of the husband's every move as she lay in his bed. Water from the kitchen tap pounded the sink basin, then attacked the metal floor of the kettle, gradually becoming muffled and high-pitched as the kettle filled up. He always filled it much more than was necessary for one cup of tea, which he seldom drank. The blow dryer. First on the highest setting, then dropped two notches to the lowest, and off. The electric razor. Whizzing up and down his cheek, circling his chin, the other cheek, grazing his neck. Snip, snip and little dark half-moon hairs from his nostrils and his sideburns cling to the rim of the white sink basin. Wiping up, scrubbing, making spotless these areas, and others, before he returns, are her evidence that she is diligent, that she is, indeed, her mother's daughter.

At this point in the routine she always expects a handsome aftershave cologne to fill the little bachelor apartment, to bring a moment of frivolity and romance into the room. In one favourite version of her memories, this is what normally happened in her parents' bedroom at precisely this point. But the husband would only pat on his face a stinging watery liquid with the faintest smell of lime, a smell that evaporated into nothingness the instant it touched his skin.

She held herself tensely, still in the crack between the bed and the wall, as he made his way into the dark corner that he called the bedroom. The folding doors of the closet squeaked open. A shirt slid off a hanger, leaving it dangling and tinkling against the metal rod. Vijai heard the shirt that she had ironed (stretched mercilessly tight across the ironing board, the tip of the iron with staccato spurts of steam sniffing out the crevice of every seam, mimicking the importance with which her mother had treated this task) being pulled against his body and his hands sliding down the stiff front as he buttoned it.

Then there was a space empty of his sounds. The silence made the walls of her stomach contract like a closed-up accordion. Her body remained rigid. Her heart sounded as if it had moved right up into her ears, thundering methodically, and that was all that she could hear. She struggled with herself to be calm so that she could know where he was and what he was doing. Not knowing made her scalp want to unpeel itself. Then, the bed sagged as he kneeled on it, leaned across and brushed his mouth on the back of her head. His full voice had no regard for her sleep or the time of morning. He said, "Happy Birthday. I left twenty dollars on the table for you. Buy yourself a present."

The thundering subsided and her heart rolled and slid, rolled and slid, down, low down, and came to rest between her thighs. She turned over with lethargic elegance, as if she were just waking up, stretching out her back like a cat, but the apartment door was already being shut and locked from the outside.

*

The streets here are so wide! I hold my breath as I walk across them, six lanes wide. What if the light changes before I get to the other side? You have to walk so briskly, not only when you're crossing a wide street but even on the sidewalk. Otherwise people pass you and then turn back and stare at you, shaking their heads. And yet I remember Mama telling us that fast walking, hurrying, was very unladylike.

I yearn for friends. My own friends, not his, but I'm afraid to smile at strangers. So often we huddled up in Mama's big bed and read the newspapers about things that happened to women up here – we read about women who suddenly disappeared and months later their corpses would be found, having been raped and dumped. And we also read about serial murders. The victims were almost always women who had been abducted from the street by strangers in some big North American city. Mama and Papa warned me, when I was leaving to come up here, not to make eye contact with strangers because I wouldn't know whose eyes I might be looking into or what I was encouraging, unknowingly. It's not like home, they said, where everybody knows everybody.

No bird sounds – there are not quite so many different kinds of birds here. Yes, Papa, yes, I can just hear you saying to stop this nonsense, all this thinking about home, that I must think of here as my home now, but I haven't yet left you and Mama. I know now that I will never fully leave, nor will I ever truly be here. You felt so close, Papa, when you phoned this morning and asked like you have every past year, how was the birthday girl. You said that in your office you often look at the calendar pictures of autumn fields of bales of hay, lazy rivers meandering near brick-red farmhouses, and country roads with quaint white wooden churches with red steeples, and you think that that's what my eyes have already enjoyed.

"It's all so beautiful, Papa," I said, and knowing you, you probably heard what I wasn't saying. Thanks for not pushing further. I couldn't tell you that he is working night and day to "make it," to "get ahead," to live like the other men he works with. That he is always thinking about this, and everything else is frivolous right now, so we haven't yet been for that drive in the country to see the pictures in the calendars pinned on the wall above your desk. He doesn't have time for dreaming, but I must dream or else I find it difficult to breathe.

At home the fence around our house and the garden was the furthest point that I ever went to on my own. From the house, winding in and out of the dracaenas and the philodendrons that I planted with Mama many Julys ago, feeling the full, firm limbs of the poui, going as far as the hibiscus and jasmine fence, and back into the house again. Any further away from the house than that and the chauffeur would be driving us! And now? Just look at me! I am out in a big city on my own. I wish you all could see me. I wish we could be doing this together.

Papa, you remember, don't you, when you used to bring home magazines from your office and I would flip through them quickly looking for full-page pictures of dense black-green tropical mountains, or snow-covered bluish-white ones? Ever since those first pictures I have dreamt of mountains, of touching them with the palms of my hands, of bicycling in them, and of hiking. Even though I never canoed on a river or a big lake with no shores, I know what it must feel like! I can feel what it is to ride rapids like they do in *National Geographic* magazines. Cold river spray and drenchings, sliding, tossing, crashing! I still dream of bicycling across a huge continent. I used to think, if only I lived in North America! But here I am, in this place where these things are supposed to happen, in the midst of so much possibility, and for some reason my dreams seem even further away, just out of reach. It's just not quite as simple as being here.

This land stretches on in front of me, behind me and forever. My back feels exposed, naked, so much land behind, and no fence ahead.

Except that I must cook dinner tonight.

What if I just kept walking and never returned! I could walk far away, to another province, change my name, cut my hair. After a while I would see my face on a poster in a grocery store, along with all the other missing persons. The problem is that then I wouldn't even be able to phone home and speak with Mama or Papa or Bindra and Vashti without being tracked and caught, and then who knows what.

Well, this is the first birthday I've ever spent alone. But next time we speak on the phone I will be able to tell you that I went for a very long walk. Alone.

I think I will do this every day – well, maybe every other day, and each time I will go a new route and a little further. I will know this place in order to own it, but still I will never really leave you.

Mama, Papa, Vashti, Bindra, Shanti,
Mama, Papa, Vashti, Bindra, Shanti.
Mama. Papa. Vashti. Bindra. Shanti.

*

Twenty-four years of Sundays, of eating three delightfully noisy, lengthy meals together, going to the beach or for long drives with big pots of rice, chicken and peas, and chocolate cake, singing "Michael Row Your Boat Ashore," and "You Are My Sunshine," doing everything in tandem with her brother and sisters and Mama and Papa. This particular characteristic of Sundays was etched deeply in her veins. (Not all Sundays were happy ones but recently she seems to have forgotten that.)

It would be her twenty-fourth Sunday here, the twenty-fourth week of marriage.

The only Sunday since the marriage that the husband had taken off and spent in his apartment was six weeks ago, and since he needed to spend that day alone Vijai agreed to go to the library for at least three hours. Before she left the house she thought she would use the opportunity to take down recipes for desserts, but once she began walking down the street she found herself thinking about rivers and mountains. She bypassed the shelves with all the cooking books and home-making magazines and found herself racing toward valleys, glaciers, canoeing, rapids and the like. She picked up a magazine about hiking and mountaineering, looked at the equipment advertisements, read incomprehensible jargon about techniques for climbing.

After about forty minutes, not seeing herself in any of the magazines, she became less enthusiastic, and eventually frustrated and bored. She looked at her watch every fifteen minutes or so and then she started watching the second hand go around and counting each and every second in her head. When three hours had passed she remembered that she had said at least three hours, and she walked home slowly, stopping to window-shop and checking her watch until an extra twenty minutes had passed.

The strength of her determination that they not spend this Sunday apart warded off even a hint of such a suggestion from the husband. What she really wanted to do was to go for the long drive up to a glacier in the nearby mountains. That way she would have him to herself for at least five hours. But he had worked several twelve-hour shifts that week and needed to rest in his apartment.

She went to the grocery store, to the gardening section, and bought half a dozen packages of flower seeds, half a dozen packages of vegetable seeds, bags of soil, fertilizer, a fork and spade, a purple plastic watering can, and a score of nursery trays. She brought it all home in a taxi. Enough to keep her busy and in his apartment for an entire Sunday. She was becoming adept at finding ways to get what she wanted.

He never asked and Vijai did not tell that from her allowance she had paid a man from the hardware store to come over and fix the balcony sliding door. She stooped on the balcony floor scooping earth into nursery trays. He sat reading the newspaper, facing the balcony in his big sagging gold armchair that he had bought next-door at a church basement sale for five dollars. She was aware that he was stealing glances at her as she bent over her garden-in-the-making.

*

I wore this shirt, no bra, am stooping, bending over here to reveal my breasts to you. *Look at them! Feel something!*

I might as well be sharing this apartment with a brother, or a roommate.

*

She feels his hands on her waist, leading her from behind to the edge of his bed. Her body is crushed under his as he slams himself against her, from behind, grunting. She holds her breath, taut against his weight and the pain, but she will not disturb his moment. She hopes that the next moment will be hers. She waits with the bed sheet pulled up to her chin. The toilet flushes and, shortly after, she hears newspaper pages being turned in the sagging five-dollar gold armchair.

Later, deep-sleep breathing and low snoring from the bedroom fills the apartment, dictating her movements. She sits on the green-and-yellow shag carpet, leaning against the foot of the husband's armchair, in front of the snowy black-and-white television watching a French station turned down low enough not to awaken him. Something about listening to a language that she does not understand comforts her, gives her companionship in a place where she feels like a foreigner. She is beginning to be able to repeat advertisements in French.

Lemon Scent

I. Paisleys in the Spaces Between

Her pale brown hands, skin fine and smooth like brushed silk, clutch an oval silver tray against her yellow sari in the area of her navel, indenting lightly. I look down at her offering – faintly wrinkled reddish black prunes. Careful not to linger to contemplate the shape of the hands, the impeccably manicured shiny-shell-pink fingernails, I concentrate, instead, on spaces between the score of healthy-looking prunes slit slightly and stuffed plump with peanut butter, the slits sealed over with firm pink icing. The spaces between the prunes reveal a white, linen-textured paper doily embossed with low relief paisleys.

The outer edge of her oval tray brushes against the area of my navel. Above the tray there is a heat growing, filling the space between her and me, and the smell of her cologne on fire thickens to fill up the space. I trace paisleys in the spaces between the prunes with my eyes.

I am careful not to imagine the warm smell of her skin, behind her ears, on the back of her neck. Grasping the tray tightly with her right hand, she obscures my paisleys with her left, fills my view with her hand. Between thumb and middle finger she picks up a prune. Her forefinger guides it from behind up toward my mouth.

I am careful not to look into her eyes.

A little shaft of light glimmers off the band of her gold wedding ring as it catches the light from another room. As her hand reaches my mouth I look over her shoulder to the other room. Her husband stands leaning against a wall sipping his drink, chatting with his friends. I barely open my mouth and her cologne rushes against the back of my throat. Her fingers touch my lips. My tongue flits against her forefinger. The heat and smell of her cologne, like a pounding surf, fill up my mind.

I am careful not to linger.

2. The Gesture of Deep Concern

He looks out the kitchen window with the phone pressed to his ear. Down the hill from that side of his house run miles and miles of undeveloped forested land – wild samaan, giant ferns, ginger lilies, bird-of-paradise bushes and palm trees, all meshed in suffocating philodendron vines – meeting the sea in the distance.

He doesn't really see what he is staring at. Level with his eyes is the horizon line where the faint sliver of white sea butts against the white sky.

His voice is distant, fading in and out of the bad telephone connection. His edges are softened with a gesture of deep concern.

" ...has everything she could ever want but ... I don't understand ... is sulking, her depression again, you know ... I am going out for some drinks with the guys from work tonight, so please come over. Spend the evening with her ... I'll be back late, very late. Spend the night. Lately she only ever laughs when she is with you ... I can count on you, can't I...? I don't want her to be unhappy.... "

He pauses, breathing in faint traces of his wife's lemon-scent-ed cologne that lingers around the mouthpiece of the phone. Reaching across meandering miles of rough country roads, the line's crackling ceases long enough for him to utter a scared, masked warning: "I must not lose her."

He hangs up the telephone, shoves his cold hands into the back pockets of his blue jeans, and absently looks out the win-dow across the rolling green lawn, dotted here and there with lone hibiscus and croton that his wife conscientiously tends, to the wire and concrete fence that surrounds his property.

He stops at the door of their bedroom before entering and anxiously watches her, his prized exquisite accomplishment, envy of his men friends, huddled in a lifeless puddle on the bed. Standing in the doorway he is not fully at ease informing her that soon he will be leaving and that he has invited Anita over to keep her company for the evening.

An image of Anita and his wife talking intently and at length, almost shyly, at a party recently, comes to his mind. She seems to sizzle with life in Anita's presence. He hopes that his gesture will charm her to him. He sees her chest flutter. Her breathing quickens noticeably.

She uncurls herself and slowly emerges from the bed. He walks over to her and reaches hopefully for her waist, but she glides in and out of his fingers before he can pull her towards him. Knots of fear are beginning to cramp his stomach. Gradual-ly his eyes harden, redden with anger.

Sitting on the edge of the bed, pulling on heavy grey-and-red sports socks, twisting and shoving his feet into greying leather running shoes, he glances up at her every few seconds.

At her dresser she stands leaning in toward the mirror, brushing her long, wavy black hair until it fluffs out light and full around her face and down her back. He has the impression that she is brushing out her hair more thoroughly than usual. He watches her face in the mirror, hoping that she will look over at his pleading face. Without taking her eyes away from her face in the mirror, she offers him a cup of tea before he leaves, but he can feel that her intention to make it is weak and unwilling.

From his stillness in the room, she knows that he is watching her as she readies herself for Anita's visit. Nervously she rambles, saying that if it rains the eaves on the roof will overflow because they need to be cleared of the leaves shedding from the poui tree in the back yard. He does not answer.

He watches her shake the bottle of lemon cologne into her hand. She rubs both hands together lightly, quickly dabs behind her ears and pats her neck, running her hands down onto her chest, the palms of her hands brushing her breasts. She pours more cologne into her hand and rubs it on the small mound of her stomach, massaging it. When she turns to walk over to her closet he gets up and crosses over to the dresser to brush his hair. Looking straight into the mirror at his own reflection, he says more loudly than is necessary, "I'm really glad that you have such a good friend in Anita."

She pulls a dress so forcefully off its hanger that the hanger springs away, snapping off the metal rod and clanging to the wooden floor. He continues, "I wonder why she isn't yet married. She is a bit of a tomboy ... not exactly appealing to a man. Do you think she is attractive?"

With her face still facing the open closet, she manages to pull up the zipper on the back of her dress by herself. He walks over to her and puts his hands on her waist. He turns her around and cups her face with his hand. With half a grin, as if cautioning her, he adds, "You know, she might be one of those types who likes only women."

He drops one hand to his side and with the other he grabs her face along her thin sharp jaw line and pulls her face up to his. Uncured sharp lemon scent settles bitterly on the back of his tongue. With his lips almost against hers he whispers, "If I ever find out that you two have slept together I will kill you both."

He presses his opened mouth onto hers, pulling her lower lip into his mouth briefly. He smooths back the hair from her face, turns and leaves.

3. Under the Samaan Tree

The dry clay earth is creamy brown, like their bodies. Underneath them a thick wool blanket, lime green, like the long thin leaves of the bird-of-paradise surrounding them, softens the ground. Their clothing is concealed in a straw bag a shade lighter than the earth. Like a fan, the edges of the densely broad-brimmed samaan dip and sway overhead, evaporating the fine beads of sweat off their bodies as fast as they form.

Kamini props herself up on her stomach and reaches a hand out to part a couple of branches of the bird-of-paradise, so that she can glimpse the house a little way off in the distance. She can see the back of the house, the top of the back stairs outside the kitchen, where she often stands looking over in this direction. (One can only find this spot if one knows where to look – behind the fence, down the steep hill with tall razor grass, a little beyond the edge of the forest to the vined, spreading samaan. From the house one can see only the top of the tree, nesting ground of hundreds of noisy parakeets.) Just behind that is where they lie.

After making love, she always parts the branches and pensively looks over to the house.

She feels Anita's palm touching her, feeling her damp skin, the shape of her arched back, fingertips skirting her bony shoulder blades. Looking at the fenced-off house in the distance, she is unable to respond like she had minutes ago to the slightest coming together of their skins. Anita sits up slightly, beginning a firmer rubbing, a more intent massaging. Kamini knows that Anita has sensed her worry.

Even though there is no one in the forest to hear them, Anita whispers, "What's happening?"

Kamini lets go of the branches, which spring back up, blocking out the house and the hill. Looking into the wall of bush she remains silent. The fermenting smell of rotting wild fruit floats over them in a wave of a cooling breeze, sharp and sweet. Anita turns to lie on her stomach and puts her arm around Kamini's back.

"What's wrong, what's going on?"

Kamini looks down at the dusty clay earth just beyond the blanket. Reddish brown leafcutter ants with young, bright green leaves in their mouths, hovering over their heads like umbrellas, march in single file back and forth over the cool ground. Black ants scurry erratically, frantically. She looks at them but does not really see them.

"He says that he'll kill us both if he ever finds out about us."

"What! Both? What do you mean? What made him suspect?"

"I don't know."

"What did you say to him?"

"Nothing."

"Do you know what made him say that? Do you think he means it?"

"I don't know. I don't know why he suspects. He just does."

Anita turns over and flops her back down; her head hits the blanket with an exaggerated thud. She clasps her hands on top of her stomach and forcefully expels a combined breath and the word "fuck!"

Kamini looks down at Anita's face, which is oddly bright, a smile taking shape on it. "What are you smiling about?"

Anita unclasps her hands and reaches up to touch Kamini's cheek.

"He's always so arrogantly flattered that those men he works with and parties with would like to have you, and so cocksure of himself that they never could. And now he's worried about me!" She grins shyly, which makes her look much younger than she is, and stares up into Kamini's face. "I just sort of like the idea that he's jealous of me, squirming about whether he has you or I do. He's probably right this minute anxiously wondering if we're somewhere making love."

"It's not something to joke about, Nita. I don't think he is joking. He would kill us if he found us together, you know! I'm really frightened that he might come looking for us."

"Does he suspect about this place?"

"I don't think so."

Anita extends her arm on the blanket, an invitation Kamini accepts, resting her forehead down on Anita's shoulder. They lie still for several seconds, then Anita pulls Kamini to rest on top of her. Their chests, stomachs and thighs are still damp. Their bodies become slippery with sweat, but gentle breezes cool them in the shade of the big tree. The branches of the samaan shift and part to reveal a thin, pale blue sky. Anita looks up distractedly, trying to catch the blue. She turns her head and whispers into Kamini's ear, "Kam, I have to ask you something. Did you sleep with him last night?"

Kamini is still.

"Tell me Kam, did you? When was the last time you slept with him?"

Kamini lifts her head and, without looking at Anita, turns to face the bird-of-paradise bush. Anita is spurred on by Kamini's silence.

"Kami, you slept with him last night, didn't you?"

"No."

"Well, when was the last time...? You did, I can tell that you did. God! I can't stand the thought of him touching you, kissing you, going and coming inside of you. How could you!"

Kamini pulls away, off onto the blanket, stiffening her body.

"What's wrong with you?" Her voice drops, sounds defeated. "I am his wife, you know! What am I supposed to do? Say no all the time? I am married to him. I can't always say no every time he wants to make love...."

Anita, hearing her sadness, tugs at her to pull her closer. Her eyes are full of tears, and Anita sits up and says coyly, "You and I make love. He and you have sex, and even once a year is too often for my liking."

"Cut it out. You make me feel as if I'm sleeping around. If I keep saying no, no, no to him, he will suspect even more strongly. You don't know him! I wouldn't put it past him to... "

Anita reaches out and touches Kamini's lips with hers, taking in the smell of skin, lips, mouth. She slides her lips around to Kamini's cheek and leaves them lightly resting there, her tongue anxious but holding back. The earthy smell of the forest, alive with decaying fruit, subsides for a moment as Anita feels herself suddenly awakening again to the familiar warm lemon scent, blunted by the evening heat, sharpened by the closeness of

Anita's breath, hovering between their faces. Kamini feels Anita responding to her smell. She lies back onto the blanket as her lover's mouth follows hers. Her fingers take time curling over Anita's shoulders, drawing her closer down as she curves her pelvis up towards Anita's. She lets Anita nestle her body between her thighs.

Kamini glances up momentarily to the top branches of the darkening samaan, bristling with lime green parakeets beginning to land for the evening, ruffling themselves, hopping around, shifting their positions. Responding to Anita, she bends her knees and gradually slides her feet up on either side of Anita's body.

The blue of the sky has turned warm yellowish white.

Wake Up

"Angenie. Angenie. Wake up."

My mother softly, urgently, calls. Her hand barely touches my shoulder before she pulls it back to herself. She doesn't have to try to wake me. I skip through the night alighting on sleep the way a butterfly barely samples petals of flowers along its path. Even though I am now fourteen I share a room with my two younger sisters, and I'm aware of every change in their breathing patterns as they sleep in their bed. Before my mother walked in I heard her coming, and in a flash I was coherent and in control.

A streetlight has lit a path through the window, across the floor and up one wall. She partially stands in its way, her face alone illuminated. It shows skin swollen with worry and loneliness, her emotions too emaciated to feel anger.

I know this pattern well, having been awakened more times than there are stars in the sky at this blackest hour of the night. Always for comfort and companionship. It would be easier if she asked for money. I could just turn my fat pink plastic pig upside down, rip off its stopper, and willingly shake it empty into her hands. But every time she comes for comforting I feel poor, and desperate to know how best to give her what she steals into my belly for. Instead I stiffen myself into emotionless calm, and take charge, duty of the night nurse.

"Where is your father, Angenie?"

She whispers, cigarette breath suspended over my face. She

has been awake long enough for worry to percolate and cause her to smoke. It calms her, to smoke. Or perhaps it is her quiet act of retaliation. If she were to find no solace, soon enough she would resort to a Scotch on-the-rocks. The first time we saw her smoke, in the dead of a night, as she sat up waiting, we played parent and scolded her to a suspiciously over-belligerent response: she was a grown woman and could do whatever she pleased.

When we first smelled alcohol on her, not the razor-sharp, sweet, racy smell of alcohol that conjures up images of revelry, but an odour made pungent and ominous because of mixing stale breath with sleeplessness and worry, I implored her not to resort to such destructive, degrading means, and Siri and Tara cried. My brother Anil's young face hardened, not toward her, but toward the unacknowledged foe, and he withdrew. After that time she would not awaken the younger ones, and would not allow me to see her smoke or drink. Never more than one cigarette or drink, mind you, and slowly, painstakingly consumed. But her bathroom, with the blue cooped-up haze, its unmistakable smell, and her breath, won't hide themselves. Her own rebellion. Asserting that, at least in her own eyes, she can maintain some modicum of power on these crazy nights when she feels less than a wife.

I cannot bear to tell her that I don't know where he is. Not that she actually expects that I would know, but I wish I could hold up a candle for her.

Not to wake up Siri and Tara, I ask back in a sliver of voice, "Daddy has not come home as yet?"

She shakes her head and purses her lips.

"What time is it?"

"It's three-fifteen. Come."

34

Come. Come into her bedroom. To sit and offer wisdom, companionship, solace. Subordination and authority given to me to juggle in the same hand like doubled-edged swords. Come. A strange demand at a time like this. It is not a request where the response might be a flower bud unfolding of itself to offer and give deliverance, but rather a command, a hand reaching into one's intestines and ripping out yard after yard, desperately searching for things it has not even defined.

Yet I get up efficiently, as if this were the time one naturally arose from bed, acutely aware that I am the chosen one in this hour of a grown-up's chaos. I hold my breath so as not to make a sound that would bring my sisters, or Anil, in his room across from ours, out of sleep, and jeopardize the coveted one-to-oneness I find myself afforded with my mother on these nights.

It is a cold night made suddenly colder. Already my neck muscles have become stiffer. My exterior, however, does not appear shaken. My mother needs me to calm her, not to encourage her fears with my own.

A little girl with a frightened mother who might just as well be blind are the only passengers in a rowboat that has a leak, tossing and tumbling about in the midst of a grey-and-silver vicious storm, clods of rapid-fire rain slashing into their eyes, the most awful crashing, cracking of the sky, and the little girl quickly deciphering the shadows of monsters lurking hungrily in the waves across the shoreless expanse of Atlantic seas. She calms and comforts and reassures her mother; she bales out water gushing up from the leak and from the waves crashing over the tiny boat; she takes off her shirt and wraps it around her mother's shoulders; she materializes a fire out of thin air to warm her poor frightened mother, and rows the boat to eventual safety, all the while taking pains to cajole the sinking morale of her mother in a voice controlled, calm and gentle.

"Where is your father? What could he be doing at this hour? I can't go on like this any longer, I do everything for you all, I've devoted my life to you all, I have never neglected my responsibilities, I've been a damn good wife, and this is what I get in return. I should have been a wife like all those other women, their husbands don't even know where they are in the middle of the day, your father does not know how lucky he is, I can't go on like this, what should I do? I only stay with your father because of you all, you know, not a damn thing has changed in these fifteen years since we got married. You're the eldest, Angenie, if only you were a boy, but I have to call on you, I am so lonely, I don't want to spend the rest of my life worrying where your father is, what am I going to do, look at my hands, they're shaking, look at my face, I am a wreck, I can't go on living like this, I just wish I could die."

I sit in the chair beside the bed, physically distanced. She sits propped against pillows in her bed, her toes curled back hard and her hands wrapping and unwrapping and wringing and unwringing a handkerchief.

She begins crying, a low wailing cry. More like a sound coming through her than from her. As if she were giving voice to all her female ancestors and they were all wailing at the same moment.

How inadequate I feel around her. Had I been, as the first offspring, a boy, I could have taken the situation more effectively in hand and offered her a strong, firm shoulder. I want to reach over and touch her, but there is no invitation. To do so would be inappropriate, not the stuff that our relationship is made of. I imagine how I would touch her if I did get the go-ahead, but to do so I must frame my protection of her in television images of the cowboy heroes I so envy.

A cowboy moves to the edge of her bed. He sits next to her on her left. He puts his right arm around her shoulders and gently draws her against him. He is a warm wall to lean into, a tall, silent man, with long hard limbs, and men fear him. He speaks no words, but she feels safe and is calmed. She knows that he will not take advantage of her. In his gentleness she feels his outrage at her hurt. He wants revenge for her.

"Mummy, don't do that to yourself. He's probably gone for a drink with the people from the meeting."

"At three-thirty? Those people have all gone home already. Whose husband is going to go drinking at this hour? Those people all have jobs that they have to get up and go to. Your father is not out at any bar. He is out with some woman."

The other times, he never even tried to hide the lipstick on the collar of his crisp white shirts or on his white handkerchiefs. She could be right this time. It almost makes one succumb to belief in the supernatural, the way she always knows where he is or what he is doing. As if she has penetrated his subconscious. Years of being burnt has taught her to infiltrate his brain and lodge herself somewhere in his psyche where she can read his every twitch and thought. She has never, however, learned to redirect him, reprogram him from the little niche she lives in inside his brain. Of what use, then, this infiltration? She at least is able to guess where he is, and so has some hook to hang on to when she can't find him on the telephone. As much as her imaginings make her fraught with anguish, having no idea whatever about where he is would be worse. Perhaps it affords her the illusion of being in control. Of not being totally in the dark.

But tonight I would prefer if she were wrong. Even if that

meant that he might come home slovenly and obnoxiously drunk. I could almost welcome him beating pots and pans at this ungodly hour when on past occasions he has insisted, with a drunk man's determination, on cooking a curry with frozen beef, for forty people. A project he would abandon halfway as alcohol-induced sleep took over. I would gratefully sleep through that commotion tonight, relieved.

But being with another woman! It was a small jump from imagining him rejecting his wife to imagining him rejecting his children. Rejecting his family. Utter chaos. Utter shame. A shame he has taught us to have. Never forget that all men are bastards, he says, and I wonder if he partly intends to include himself in the pronouncement of this simple truth, and so to excuse himself for being one. But I, family, automatically exempt him from this.

A flash of loathing rises up in me and instantly subsides as it meets a wall that wills him to be out drinking.

"Mommy, you're letting your imagination run away with you. I can understand why you think he is with someone else, but I am sure, as sure as you are about where he is, that he is only out having a few drinks. He is probably not doing anything wrong. He just has a lot of worries and needs to go out and forget them for a while. He works so hard and then he goes to meetings. He never has time for relaxing. And if he comes home we all want help with homework. People are always phoning, are always coming. He needs a little time of his own. You're worrying yourself for nothing."

Her face has changed. She seems reassured, and leans back a little more relaxed. And I find myself praying to the stars that I am right. If I am right we will remain a family intact. If I am right she will call on me again. How easily she believes anything that makes her feel better.

Almost four in the morning. I have to get up for school in two hours.

Suddenly she is out of bed and lunging at the bathroom light to turn it off. Nervously she hurries back into bed.

"Listen! He is here. Go on back to bed quickly."

I still cannot hear the car so I hesitate, listening. I hear nothing.

"What are you waiting for? I said go to bed. Do you want him to come in and catch us awake? You know how badly he will behave if he is drunk. Go to bed."

Catch us. As if we were the ones at fault. Once he came home hours after midnight and found us waiting up, worried, and he behaved as if that act were itself an accusation.

And now I hear the low hum at the gate. How well her ears know the sound of his car from so far away. From all the nights she has sat alone in the dark and picked it out above the rustling of the coconut trees, and amongst the other cars on the highway.

In a voice sharpened with fear she snaps, "Go!" And I know that my position is subordinate again. I go.

In the darkness I see that Siri's eyes are open. Light from the corridor bounces off the whites of her eyes in little beams. We do not speak to each other. I wonder if Tara, in the same bed, and Anil in his room, are also awake in their dark corners, aware of everything. I feel a flicker of disgust that they did not come to our mother's rescue when she most wanted it. And then arrogant pride that I am the one who could be counted on in an emergency.

I slip into bed noiselessly, and hold my breath. I cover my face with my arm so that my shut eyes would not be seen flickering in fright in case my father were to look in on us.

His footsteps are sure, not those of a drinking man. Perhaps the meeting was indeed a very long one. Faint sounds of hushed, clipped talking come from my parents' room. Relieved at the thought of quiet in the remaining hours of dark, I relax, and drift quickly toward sleep.

A coconut estate. Near a fence. Three of us lie on the uncovered ground of crabgrass and dried coconut branches. In a window of a house outside the fence, the upper body of a man paces back and forth. He is unaware of us, but I am anxious that he might look over and see us. The girl lying on my right talks incessantly. I do not know what she is saying. On my left is a person, older, female. My body gathers heat from hers. I wish the girl on my right would leave us alone. I wish so hard that she disappears. Now we are alone. The fingers of my left hand fall open and touch the woman's skirt. I want to hold her. I want her to hold me. My heart beats a ferocious tune.

The man in the window paces, unaware. I roll onto one elbow and move my face towards hers. Slowly my mouth is lowered onto hers. Her lips press back onto mine, but only so briefly that I am left standing outside of myself looking at us, wishing to know more. And then, suddenly, she has turned away. My own desires insist on being heard but no amount of begging and tugging will bring her back. I am afraid that she might even be dead. Her face becomes recognizable; it is my mother's, and seeing this, I demand with the power of an impetuous, desperate kiss that she not desert me.

Siri and Tara are up and almost dressed for school when I open my eyes. My heart is racing and I can feel the muscles of my face contorted by the passion and pain of a kiss, a kiss that is fast evaporating. Colours and details of my dream have begun to fade

40

but my chest holds tangled, knotted vestiges of grief, and pleasure, of moments of invincibility, and terror; confusions that could be assuaged by that kiss.

Bring back the kiss....

Until I remember that the face of the woman was my mother's.

How could I possibly have dreamt this! Perhaps I was mistaken; it was not my mother whom I kissed. But I recall the dream, and hard as I try I cannot replace her face with someone else's. The chaos in my chest abruptly gels to expose a singular shame. Worst of all is that such a dream would come out of me mere hours after I was privy to her brittleness.

I cover my face with the blanket and wonder what kind of a monster I am. How can I face her? She is bound to know when she sees me.

"Angenie. Do you realize what time it is? It's ten to seven. You're going to be late for school. Get up!"

My mother stands over me. The skin of her face is puffy, awake-all-night skin. Her tired, heavy eyes, and mouth taut at the ends, contain a crying, fighting rage. She looks like a rope stretched so tightly that it is about to snap. She is not aware of my dream. Commanding me to get up for school, she attempts to sever any bond from last night.

Looking at her face I try to see in it a person with whom I could have enjoyed even the less odious act of hugging. I am pleased that I have not the remotest desire for her. Repulsion (the less damning edge of guilt) for kissing my mother, even if it was only in a dream, follows me around as I get up and prepare for school. Where do dreams come from? What inside of me could have created such a dream?

"Where was Daddy last night?" I ask, forcing her to acknowledge that she had broken down in front of me only hours ago. Yet I know full well that she will give only enough of an answer to justify her angst, and brush away admission of my father's slight toward her. Now, in the light of day, her bravery does not need propping, and she will not tolerate any hint of criticism of him.

"He says the meeting was late."

"Do you believe him?"

She bites the corner of her lower lip and curtly replies, "No."

I don't want to overstep my boundaries by asking where she thinks he was. What I feel for her this morning is decidedly not desire, not even the desire of a cowboy to protect her, but disgust. Last night when she opened her wounds for me to see, and when she asked me to wait up with her, I would have climbed mountains to deliver her. But this morning, as she denies me, I despise her for spinelessness. For cringing in the face of my father's philandering. I despise her role of excellent wife who stands behind the successful husband, of mother of polite, well-behaved and smart schoolchildren. I despise her for staying, for the way she allows herself to be hurt, the way she accepts it.

The woman before me and the woman I kissed in my dream have the same features but my feelings toward them are vastly different.

Being female, my future looks grim, claustrophobic. I worry that I am expected, as a girl, to grow up to be just like her. The alternative to being just like her is to be just like him. And as much as I cry inside at his rejection of her and so of us, his freedom looks more exciting, interesting. The freedom to work, to go to meetings, to speak his mind; the freedom to go out with the "boys" until way into the early morning hours, to smoke, to drink, to have adventures. The freedom, inherent in his maleness, to philander. What he does with the freedom is another matter. Still, the fantasy of modelling myself in his image (with modifications to the details, mind you) is more honourable than consenting to spending a lifetime trapped by the body of a female.

If I were afforded such independence I would see the world, ride a bicycle from Alaska to Tierra Del Fuego, hike in Bhutan, snorkel above the Great Barrier Reef, befriend Prince Charles, wrestle with him at polo, and then later that day talk with him about great world architecture. I would make paintings like the one of Dorian Gray. I would write like Somerset Maugham. I would disguise myself as a boy and one would never know that I was a girl.

Besides obvious fear, the mere thought of Mummy fills me with sadness. I no longer expect to be able to please her, and passively accept this. But, even though it seems impossible to do, I have an unquenchable thirst for pleasing Daddy. His boldness and bravery are intimidating. I am afraid of him and admire him. I am cautious to loathe his actions, not him.

I have not seen him this morning as yet. I am avoiding him. It is time to leave for school and I must say good-bye to them both.

But I can hardly look him in his eyes. Perhaps I'd rather not see evidence of his rejection of us, of another woman in his smile or in his voice. What did he do with her last night? Did he kiss her? Did my father touch her breasts? Did he lie down with her? Did she hold his face in her hands, did he do to her what he does with Mummy? There is no enjoyment in this!

I hardly hear what is being taught at school today. For one thing, I am unbearably tired. For another, I have pictures in my head of my mother lying in bed crying; of my father making love to a plethora of strange women; of a jealous woman poisoning her husband; of a raging madwoman stabbing herself and her children; of a cowboy bringing his wagon and putting the woman and her children in it and riding off with them to a sprawling homestead in the country, far away from other people.

Out on Main Street

I.

Janet and me? We does go Main Street to see pretty pretty sari and bangle, and to eat we belly full a burfi and gulub jamoon, but we doh go too often because, yuh see, is dem sweets self what does give people like we a presupposition for untameable hip and thigh.

Another reason we shy to frequent dere is dat we is watered-down Indians – we ain't good grade A Indians. We skin brown, is true, but we doh even think 'bout India unless something happen over dere and it come on de news. Mih family remain Hindu ever since mih ancestors leave India behind, but nowadays dey doh believe in praying unless things real bad, because, as mih father always singing, like if is a mantra: "Do good and good will be bestowed unto you." So he is a veritable saint cause he always doing good by his women friends and dey chilren. I sure some a dem must be mih half sister and brother, oui!

Mostly, back home, we is kitchen Indians: some kind a Indian food every day, at least once a day, but we doh get cardamom and other fancy spice down dere so de food not spicy like Indian food I eat in restaurants up here. But it have one thing we doh make joke 'bout down dere: we like we meethai and sweetrice too much, and it remain overly authentic, like de day Naana and Naani step off de boat in Port of Spain harbour over a hundred and sixty years ago. Check out dese hips here nah, dey is pure sugar and condensed milk, pure sweetness!

But Janet family different. In de ole days when Canadian missionaries land in Trinidad dey used to make a bee-line straight for Indians from down South. And Janet great grandparents is one a de first South families dat exchange over from Indian to Presbyterian. Dat was a long time ago.

When Janet born, she father, one Mr. John Mahase, insist on asking de Reverend MacDougal from Trace Settlement Church, a leftover from de Canadian Mission, to name de baby girl. De good Reverend choose de name Constance cause dat was his mother name. But de mother a de child, Mrs. Savitri Mahase, wanted to name de child sheself. Ever since Savitri was a lil girl she like de yellow hair, fair skin and pretty pretty clothes Janet and John used to wear in de primary school reader – since she lil she want to change she name from Savitri to Janet but she own father get vex and say how Savitri was his mother name and how she will insult his mother if she gone and change it. So Savitri get she own way once by marrying this fella name John, and she do a encore, by calling she daughter Janet, even doh husband John upset for days at she for insulting de good Reverend by throwing out de name a de Reverend mother.

So dat is how my girlfriend, a darkskin Indian girl with thick black hair (pretty fuh so!) get a name like Janet.

She come from a long line a Presbyterian school teacher, headmaster and headmistress. Savitri still teaching from de same Janet and John reader in a primary school in San Fernando, and John, getting more and more obtuse in his ole age, is headmaster more dan twenty years now in Princes Town Boys' Presbyterian High School. Everybody back home know dat family good good. Dat is why Janet leave in two twos. Soon as A Level finish she pack up and take off like a jet plane so she could live without people only shoo-shooing behind she back ... "But A A! Yuh ain't hear de goods 'bout John Mahase daughter, gyul? How yuh mean yuh ain't hear? Is a big thing! Everybody talking 'bout she. Hear dis, nah! Yuh ever see she wear a dress? Yes! Doh look at mih so. Yuh reading mih right!"

Is only recentish I realize Mahase is a Hindu last name. In de ole days every Mahase in de country turn Presbyterian and now de name doh have no association with Hindu or Indian whatsoever. I used to think of it as a Presbyterian Church name until some days ago when we meet a Hindu fella fresh from India name Yogdesh Mahase who never even hear of Presbyterian.

De other day I ask Janet what she know 'bout Divali. She say, "It's the Hindu festival of lights, isn't it?" like a line straight out a dictionary. Yuh think she know anything 'bout how lord Rama get himself exile in a forest for fourteen years, and how when it come time for him to go back home his followers light up a pathway to help him make his way out, and dat is what Divali lights is all about? All Janet know is 'bout going for drive in de country to see light, and she could remember looking forward, around Divali time, to the lil brown paper-bag packages full a burfi and parasad that she father Hindu students used to bring for him.

One time in a Indian restaurant she ask for parasad for dessert. Well! Since den I never go back in dat restaurant, I embarrass fuh so!

I used to think I was a Hindu *par excellence* until I come up here and see real flesh and blood Indian from India. Up here, I learning 'bout all kind a custom and food and music and clothes dat we never see or hear 'bout in good ole Trinidad. Is de next best thing to going to India, in truth, oui! But Indian store clerk on Main Street doh have no patience with us, specially when we talking English to dem. Yuh ask dem a question in English and dey insist on giving de answer in Hindi or Punjabi or Urdu or Gujarati. How I suppose to know de difference even! And den dey look at yuh disdainful disdainful – like yuh disloyal, like yuh is a traitor.

But yuh know, it have one other reason I real reluctant to go Main Street. Yuh see, Janet pretty fuh so! And I doh like de way men does look at she, as if because she wearing jeans and T-shirt and high-heel shoe and make-up and have long hair loose and flying about like she is a walking-talking shampoo ad, dat she easy. And de women always looking at she beady eye, like she loose and going to thief dey man. Dat kind a thing always make me want to put mih arm round she waist like, she is my woman, take yuh eyes off she! and shock de false teeth right out dey mouth. And den is a whole other story when dey see me with mih crew cut and mih blue jeans tuck inside mih jim-boots. Walking next to Janet, who so femme dat she redundant, tend to make me look like a gender dey forget to classify. Before going Main Street I does parade in front de mirror practicing a jiggly-wiggly kind a walk. But if I ain't walking like a strong-man monkey I doh exactly feel right and I always revert back to mih true colours. De men dem does look at me like if dey is exactly what I need a taste of to cure me good and proper. I could see dey eyes watching Janet and me, dey face growing dark as dey imagining all kind a situation and position. And de women dem embarrass fuh so to watch me in mih eye, like dey fraid I will jump up and try to kiss dem, or make pass at dem. Yuh know, sometimes I wonder if I ain't mad enough to do it just for a little bacchanal, nah!

Going for a outing with mih Janet on Main Street ain't easy! If only it wasn't for burfi and gulub jamoon! If only I had a learned how to cook dem kind a thing before I leave home and come up here to live!

2.

In large deep-orange Sanskrit-style letters, de sign on de saffron-colour awning above de door read "Kush Valley Sweets." Underneath in smaller red letters it had "Desserts Fit For The Gods." It was a corner building. The front and side was one big glass wall. Inside was big. Big like a gymnasium. Yuh could see in through de brown tint windows: dark brown plastic chair, and brown table, each one de length of a door, line up stiff and straight in row after row like if is a school room.

Before entering de restaurant I ask Janet to wait one minute outside with me while I rumfle up mih memory, pulling out all de sweet names I know from home, besides burfi and gulub jamoon: meethai, jilebi, sweetrice (but dey call dat kheer up here), and ladhoo. By now, of course, mih mouth watering fuh so! When I feel confident enough dat I wouldn't make a fool a mih Brown self by asking what dis one name? and what dat one name? we went in de restaurant. In two twos all de spice in de place take a flying leap in our direction and give us one big welcome hug up, tight fuh so! Since den dey take up permanent residence in de jacket I wear dat day!

Mostly it had women customers sitting at de tables, chatting and laughing, eating sweets and sipping masala tea. De only men in de place was de waiters, and all six waiters was men. I figure dat dey was brothers, not too hard to conclude, because all a dem had de same full round chin, round as if de chin stretch tight over a ping-pong ball, and dey had de same big roving eyes. I know better dan to think dey was mere waiters in de employ of a owner who chook up in a office in de back. I sure dat dat was dey own family business, dey stomach proudly preceeding dem and dey shoulders throw back in de confidence of dey ownership.

It ain't dat I paranoid, yuh understand, but from de moment we enter de fellas dem get over-animated, even armorously agitated. Janet again! All six pair a eyes land up on she, following she every move and body part. Dat in itself is something dat does madden me, oui! but also a kind a irrational envy have a tendency to manifest in me. It was like I didn't exist. Sometimes it could be a real problem going out with a good-looker, yes! While I ain't remotely interested in having a squeak of a flirtation with a man, it doh hurt a ego to have a man notice yuh once in a very long while. But with Janet at mih side, I doh have de chance of a penny shave-ice in de hot sun. I tuck mih elbows in as close to mih sides as I could so I wouldn't look like a strong man next to she, and over to de l-o-n-g glass case jam up with sweets I jiggle and wiggle in mih best imitation a some a dem gay fellas dat I see downtown Vancouver, de ones who more femme dan even Janet. I tell she not to pay de brothers no attention, because if any a dem flirt with she I could start a fight right dere and den. And I didn't feel to mess up mih crew cut in a fight.

De case had sweets in every nuance of colour in a rainbow. Sweets I never before see and doh know de names of. But dat was alright because I wasn't going to order dose ones anyway.

Since before we leave home Janet have she mind set on a nice thick syrupy curl a jilebi and a piece a plain burfi so I order dose for she and den I ask de waiter-fella, resplendent with thick thick bright-yellow gold chain and ID bracelet, for a stick a meethai for mihself. I stand up waiting by de glass case for it but de waiter/owner lean up on de back wall behind de counter watching me like he ain't hear me. So I say loud enough for him, and every body else in de room to hear, "I would like to have one piece a meethai please," and den he smile and lift up his hands, palms open-out motioning across de vast expanse a glass case, and he say, "Your choice! Whichever you want, Miss." But he still lean up against de back wall grinning. So I stick mih head out and up like a turtle and say louder, and slowly, "One piece a meethai – dis one!" and I point sharp to de stick a flour mix with ghee, deep fry and den roll up in sugar. He say, "That is koorma, Miss. One piece only?"

Mih voice drop low all by itself. "Oh ho! Yes, one piece. Where I come from we does call dat meethai." And den I add, but only loud enough for Janet to hear, "And mih name ain't 'Miss.'"

He open his palms out and indicate de entire panorama a sweets and he say, "These are all meethai, Miss. Meethai is Sweets. Where are you from?"

I ignore his question and to show him I undaunted, I point to a round pink ball and say, "I'll have one a dese sugarcakes too please." He start grinning broad broad like if he half-pitying, half-laughing at dis Indian-in-skin-colour-only, and den he tell me, "That is called chum-chum, Miss." I snap back at him, "Yeh, well back home we does call dat sugarcake, Mr. Chum-chum."

At de table Janet say, "You know, Pud [Pud, short for Pud-ding; is dat she does call me when she feeling close to me, or sorry for me], it's true that we call that 'meethai' back home. Just like how we call 'siu mai' 'tim sam.' As if 'dim sum' is just one lit-tle piece a food. What did he call that sweet again?"

"Cultural bastards, Janet, cultural bastards. Dat is what we is.

Yuh know, one time a fella from India who living up here call me a bastardized Indian because I didn't know Hindi. And now look at dis, nah! De thing is: all a we in Trinidad is cultural bastards, Janet, all a we. *Toutes bagailles!* Chinese people, Black people, White people. Syrian. Lebanese. I looking forward to de day I find out dat place inside me where I am nothing else but Trinidadian, whatever dat could turn out to be."

I take a bite a de chum-chum, de texture was like grind-up coconut but it had no coconut, not even a hint a coconut taste in it. De thing was juicy with sweet rose water oozing out a it. De rose water perfume enter mih nose and get trap in mih cranium. Ah drink two cup a masala tea and a lassi and still de rose water perfume was on mih tongue like if I had a overdosed on Butchart Gardens.

Suddenly de door a de restaurant spring open wide with a strong force and two big burly fellas stumble in, almost rolling over on to de ground. Dey get up, eyes red and slow and dey skin burning pink with booze. Dey straighten up so much to over-compensate for falling forward, dat dey find deyself leaning backward. Everybody stop talking and was watching dem. De guy in front put his hand up to his forehead and take a deep Walter Raleigh bow, bringing de hand down to his waist in a rolling circular movement. Out loud he greet everybody with "Alarm o salay koom." A part a me wanted to bust out laughing. Another part make mih jaw drop open in disbelief. De calm in de place get rumfle up. De two fellas dem, feeling chupid now because nobody reply to dey greeting, gone up to de counter to Chum-chum trying to make a little conversation with him. De same booze-pink alarm-o-salay-koom-fella say to Chum-chum, "Hey, howaryah?"

Chum-Chum give a lil nod and de fella carry right on, "Are

you Sikh?"

Chum-chum brothers converge near de counter, busying dey-selves in de vicinity. Chum-chum look at his brothers kind a quizzical, and he touch his cheek and feel his forehead with de back a his palm. He say, "No, I think I am fine, thank you. But I am sorry if I look sick, Sir."

De burly fella confuse now, so he try again.

"Where are you from?"

Chum-chum say, "Fiji, Sir."

"Oh! Fiji, eh! Lotsa palm trees and beautiful women, eh! Is it true that you guys can have more than one wife?"

De exchange make mih blood rise up in a boiling froth. De restaurant suddenly get a gruff quietness 'bout it except for a woman I hear whispering angrily to another woman at de table behind us, "I hate this! I just hate it! I can't stand to see our men humiliated by them, right in front of us. He should refuse to serve them, he should throw them out. Who on earth do they think they are? The awful fools!" And de friend whisper back, "If he throws them out all of us will suffer in the long run."

I could discern de hair on de back a de neck a Chum-chum brothers standing up, annoyed, and at de same time de brothers look like dey was shrinking in stature. Chum-chum get serious, and he politely say, "What can I get for you?"

Pinko get de message and he point to a few items in de case and say, "One of each, to go please."

Holding de white take-out box in one hand he extend de other to Chum-chum and say, "How do you say 'Excuse me, I'm sorry' in Fiji?"

Chum-chum shake his head and say, "It's okay. Have a good day."

Pinko insist, "No, tell me please. I think I just behaved badly, and I want to apologize. How do you say 'I'm sorry' in Fiji?"

Chum-chum say, "Your apology is accepted. Everything is okay." And he discreetly turn away to serve a person who had just entered de restaurant. De fellas take de hint dat was broad like daylight, and back out de restaurant like two little mouse.

Everybody was feeling sorry for Chum-chum and Brothers. One a dem come up to de table across from us to take a order from a woman with a giraffe-long neck who say, "Brother, we mustn't accept how these people think they can treat us. You men really put up with too many insults and abuse over here. I really felt for you."

Another woman gone up to de counter to converse with Chum-chum in she language. She reach out and touch his hand, sympathy-like. Chum-chum hold the one hand in his two and make a verbose speech to her as she nod she head in agreement generously. To italicize her support, she buy a take-out box a two burfi, or rather, dat's what I think dey was.

De door a de restaurant open again, and a bevy of Indian-looking women saunter in, dress up to weaken a person's decorum. De Miss Universe pageant traipse across de room to a table. Chum-chum and Brothers start smoothing dey hair back, and pushing de front a dey shirts neatly into dey pants. One brother take out a pack a Dentyne from his shirt pocket and pop one in his mouth. One take out a comb from his back pocket and smooth down his hair. All a dem den converge on dat single table to take orders. Dey begin to behave like young pups in mating season. Only, de women dem wasn't impress by all this tra-la-la at all and ignore dem except to make dey order, straight to de point. Well, it look like Brothers' egos were having a rough day and dey start roving 'bout de room, dey egos and de crotch a dey pants leading far in front dem. One brother gone over to

Giraffebai to see if she want anything more. He call she "dear" and put his hand on she back. Giraffebai straighten she back in surprise and reply in a not-too-friendly way. When he gone to write up de bill she see me looking at she and she say to me, "Whoever does he think he is! Calling me dear and touching me like that! Why do these men always think that they have permission to touch whatever and wherever they want! And you can't make a fuss about it in public, because it is exactly what those people out there want to hear about so that they can say how sexist and uncivilized our culture is."

I shake mih head in understanding and say, "Yeah. I know. Yuh right!"

De atmosphere in de room take a hairpin turn, and it was man aggressing on woman, woman warding off a herd a man who just had dey pride publicly cut up a couple a times in just a few minutes.

One brother walk over to Janet and me and he stand up facing me with his hands clasp in front a his crotch, like if he protecting it. Stiff stiff, looking at me, he say, "Will that be all?"

Mih crew cut start to tingle, so I put on mih femmest smile and say, "Yes, that's it, thank you. Just the bill please." De smartass turn to face Janet and he remove his hands from in front a his crotch and slip his thumbs inside his pants like a cowboy 'bout to do a square dance. He smile, looking down at her attentive fuh so, and he say, "Can I do anything for you?"

I didn't give Janet time fuh his intent to even register before I bulldoze in mih most un-femmest manner, "She have everything she need, man, thank you. The bill please." Yuh think he hear me? It was like I was talking to thin air. He remain smiling at Janet, but she, looking at me, not at him, say, "You heard her. The bill please."

Before he could even leave de table proper, I start mih tirade. "But A A! Yuh see dat? Yuh could believe dat! De effing so-and-so! One minute yuh feel sorry fuh dem and next minute dey harassing de heck out a you. Janet, he crazy to mess with my woman, yes!" Janet get vex with me and say I overreacting, and is not fuh me to be vex, but fuh she to be vex. Is she he insult, and she could take good enough care a sheself.

I tell she I don't know why she don't cut off all dat long hair, and stop wearing lipstick and eyeliner. Well, who tell me to say dat! She get real vex and say dat nobody will tell she how to dress and how not to dress, not me and not any man. Well I could see de potential dat dis fight had coming, and when Janet get fighting vex, watch out! It hard to get a word in edgewise, yes! And she does bring up incidents from years back dat have no bearing on de current situation. So I draw back quick quick but she don't waste time; she was already off to a good start. It was best to leave right dere and den.

Just when I stand up to leave, de doors dem open up and in walk Sandy and Lise, coming for dey weekly hit a Indian sweets. Well, with Sandy and Lise is a dead giveaway dat dey not dressing fuh any man, it have no place in dey life fuh man-vibes, and dat in fact dey have a blatant penchant fuh women. Soon as dey enter de room yuh could see de brothers and de couple men customers dat had come in minutes before stare dem down from head to Birkenstocks, dey eyes bulging with disgust. And de women in de room start shoo-shooing, and putting dey hand in front dey mouth to stop dey surprise, and false teeth, too, from falling out. Sandy and Lise spot us instantly and dey call out to us, shameless, loud and affectionate. Dey leap over to us, eager to hug up and kiss like if dey hadn't seen us for years, but it was really only since two nights aback when we went out to dey favourite Indian restaurant for dinner. I figure dat de display was a genuine happiness to be seen wit us in dat place. While we stand up dere chatting, Sandy insist on rubbing she hand up and down Janet back – wit friendly intent, mind you, and same time Lise have she arm round Sandy waist. Well, all cover get blown. If it was even remotely possible dat I wasn't noticeable before, now Janet and I were over-exposed. We could a easily suffer from hypothermia, specially since it suddenly get cold cold in dere. We say goodbye, not soon enough, and as we were leaving I turn to acknowledge Giraffebai, but instead a any recognition of our buddiness against de fresh brothers, I get a face dat look like it was in de presence of a very foul smell.

De good thing, doh, is dat Janet had become so incensed 'bout how we get scorned, dat she forgot I tell she to cut she hair and to ease up on de make-up, and so I get save from hearing 'bout how I too jealous, and how much I inhibit she, and how she would prefer if I would grow *my* hair, and wear lipstick and put on a dress sometimes. I so glad, oui! dat I didn't have to go through hearing how I too demanding a she, like de time, she say, I prevent she from seeing a ole boyfriend when he was in town for a couple hours *en route* to live in Australia with his new bride (because, she say, I was jealous dat ten years ago dey sleep together.) Well, look at mih crosses, nah! Like if I really so possessive and jealous!

So tell me, what yuh think 'bout dis nah, girl?

Sushila's Bhakti

(for Shauna Beharry)

Sushila unplugged the telephone and locked herself in her studio. A roughly torn piece of white bristol board marked "Do Not Disturb" in thick black marker was pinned to the door.

She sat with her back upright, recalling the one class of beginners' meditation yoga she had taken a few years ago at the community centre. She placed her hands palm down on her lap, and held her legs loosely together. First her cheeks relaxed, then she let fall her lower jaw. Next she let her head rest itself on the top of her spine, instead of rigidly holding it up. Layers of concrete fell off her neck, shoulders and upper arms. There was no one around to watch her stomach expand and sag. She let go of the muscles in her bum, permitting it to spread over the seat of the chair. She took a slow, leisurely breath and was surprised at how deeply she could inhale. When she exhaled her relaxation deepened, spreading over her in caterpillar-like progression.

"God. Beauty. Truth." She paused between the words, not thinking about them, but rather feeling their meaning in her chest, in her heart. From the pores of her skin.

"Absolute Truth.

Godness. Honesty. Nowness.

The Face of Godness.

Absolute Beauty,

Truth that is in me and in everything."

She raised her hands, palms opened upward, gesturing to the

canvas-stretcher covered with burlap from a basmati rice bag and said, "This is my *bhakti*." Her grandmother would have been proud, but baffled too. She got up, and began opening the plastic bags of mendhi. They cost $3.99. Cheaper than paint, she thought, and quickly focused back on her act of *bhakti*.

She had learnt the word only days ago. Devotion. Love. Not of or for worldly things, but of the Pure, True, Self. Big "S." What some people call God. She couldn't bring herself to pray to an all-seeing, all-knowing, all-powerful God. And a male one too. That would have made her feel too much like a puppet, out of her own control, co-dependent. So the concept of S(s)elf – big "S," little "s" – made much more sense.

They were Brahmins, her grandmother used to repeat proudly. But back in those days when she was a child, all that meant was restrictions, expectations, big "O" Obligations. She had to be a "goodBrahmingirl," no loose behaviour, which over the course of time and admonishments she learned to identify. And, definitely, no taking part in carnival.

The grandmother simply did not know how to or why she should follow her son, Sushila's father, when he stepped horizontally out of his caste, into the upper crust of British-influenced colonial Trinidad society. Caste = class. Brahmin lost its religious meaning for all but the grandmother, who dug her feet in deeper to teach her grandchildren the Hindi alphabet and to read to them from the Bhagavad Gita. Eventually they became utterly confused, when even she, submitting to national cultural chaos, would tuck them into bed, clasp their hands in front of their chests and have them repeat after her a prayer from a little book given to her by a stranger who had come to the house to invite her and her household to his church: "Now I lay me down to sleep, I pray the Lord my soul to keep. If I should die before I wake, I pray the Lord my soul to take."

Having Brahmin roots somewhere deep in her, Sushila knew she had buried connections to that higher Self, connections that could be excavated and polished up. She would embark on a revival of her distant past to take control of her present.

For ten years she had been floating rootlessly in the Canadian landscape, not properly Trinidadian (she could not sing one calypso, or shake down her hips with abandon when one was sung – the diligence of being a goodBrahmingirl), not Indian except in skin colour (now, curries and too many spices gave her frightful cramps, and the runs, and in her family a sari had always been a costume), certainly not White and hardly Canadian either. Except in the sense that Canada was a country full of rootless and floating people.

After Sushila's first exhibition, ten years ago, at the N!O!W! Gallery, a reviewer wrote that her style was "delightfully naive," and talked of her "refreshing folksy crudeness." In reaction, out of desire to be an authentic Canadian painter, she removed folksy decoration, borders and patterning from her work, and toned down her naive "tropical" colour. She painted large temperate-zone fruit and immense cold-country vegetables, with broad, sweeping, gestural strokes in imitation of the size, depth, feel, colour and temperature of the Canadian landscape. Her heart and shoulders sagged. Colour went out of her life.

She had never touched mendhi before. When it fell out of the pack in a clump of powder, a fine, olive-green dust floated up. It jogged her memory. She recognised the smell, the most powerful of memory stimulants. She couldn't identify it, knew even that her memory was not from this lifetime. Mendhi was not a part of her Indo-Trinidadian past.

That kind of thought would once have saddened her. Now it angers her. From day to day, her skin colour being her primary identifier, she is constantly reminded by certain others of her Indian past. Not by Indians born and bred in India, who insist defiantly that she is in fact not truly Indian (adding to her rootless and confused floating), but by certain others. Brown equals Indian equals India, they had carelessly assumed. So how come, these certain others want to know, she is so ignorant of things Indian? And she becomes angered by the answers. "Indians stem from India, even if they weren't born there, or their parents either. That is where their roots lie." This logic has become inscribed on her fast-obliterating self-image. She wants to know why it is that all that she has of her Indian heritage are her name, Sushila, and her skin colour, both of which are like lies about her identity. She yearns for an understanding that digs deeper than the well-known facts of British Will and Empire.

Sushila's friend Ravi, who lives in Toronto, brought his new bride to Vancouver for their honeymoon. It was her first trip outside of India. She spoke English well but with no confidence. Sushila gawked in awe and curiosity at the bride's yellow hands and feet decorated with brown dots that, when connected dot to dot, formed patterns, borders and flowers: "Mendhi. Pithi. You mix with water, and little oil. Then put on, then take off."

Sushila made a well in the centre of the mendhi lying in a mound on the stretched rice bag, and in an act of bhakti she filled the well with water. She launched her hands into it the way she remembered her grandmother back home in Trinidad beginning to knead flour and water for roti. Sushila juggled the experience of this new sensation and of imitating her Brahmin grandmother (not the action only, but the ritual devotion to family, the preparing of sustenance for their body and soul – fulfilling, according to her father, the duty of woman and mother – that transported her beyond her grandmother to her earliest ancestors).

She poured linseed oil onto the mixture and felt it become smoother under her kneading. The whole consistency began to take a different shape in her memory.

Pundit Maharaj in his white dhoti and kurta preparing for an afternoon pooja at Sushila's parents' home, a shallow square wooden box packed tight and smooth, decorating it with ... what was it decorated with? She summoned up her early childhood memories and came up with white flour, and coloured rice dribbled to create a border and patterns, the petals of the hibiscus flower, and deep green mango leaves in a bright and shiny brass container. And the swastika! Ah, that swastika, symbol of life and celebration before it was stolen, tipped over and further sullied.

Priests, pundits, were men, she thought. Brahmin men, not women. But Sushila was getting wise to a time before his-story wiped out her-story, when women ruled, and were the spiritual guides, and mediums. Sushila became, right there and then, a Brahmin woman pundit kneading and packing earth into a pooja box. Using the mendhi was like having a fine poetic substitute for earth. Suddenly using earth for one's devotion lost its primitiveness and she experienced a moment of completeness, oneness with the universe, a feeling unlike any she'd experienced when she'd tried on Catholicism, or TM, or gone vegetarian in an effort to find a lasting identity and purpose.

She had glimpsed the core of her identity. This act of art-making was itself an expression of her bhakti.

Poly-fix threatened the sanctity of the previous moment, but it was needed for its adhesion quality – otherwise the mendhi would dry, crack and flake off. It also stretched and elasticized the mendhi mixture. The compound smelled like spiced earth.

"The Brits invaded India." She kneaded the mixture more fiercely, more passionately. "Stole its heart and soul. Juggled and shuffled our conquered people all over their empire, disregarding traditions, cultures and souls. The Brits, they inveaded Trinidad. My great grands ended up in Trinidad to work the Brits' sugarcane fields because the enslaved Blacks ran as far away as their leashes would take them from the vehicles of slavery."

Brown skin, the purest legacy left to Indians generations away from India. And yet, whenever some ignoramus breathed out "Paki, Punjab," as she walked by, Sushila thought how wrong they were. A tame response, but that kind of ignorance simply baffled her into inaction. She had been called Hindu before, too – meant as an insult – but because it was a fact, she was stumped here also, unable to dispute it. People like her were neither here nor there. Roots diluted, language lost. Religion held onto only by the thin straps of festivals.

Sushila took fistfuls of the mixture and squeezed it slowly so that it oozed out between her fingers. She began to spread it smoothly over the rice bag, erasing the blue, red and green design:

DEHRADOON NO. 1, BASMATEE RICE. GUARANTEED BEST.
IMPORTED BY HANIF'S INTERNATIONAL FOODS LTD.
RICHMOND, B.C.

"I want to connect with my point of origin. Not the point of origin as in 'Who-made-me-God-made-me,' nor the point at which we are said to have flipped over from animal to human, but rather the origin of Indian-ness. Where the heck did the Indians in India come from anyway? They were in India, I'm told, for a long enough time that the question is pointless (isn't Hinduism the oldest religion in the world?). But didn't the majority of these Indians originate from someplace else, in the West? This majority, weren't they once themselves White(ish) folks who invaded the Indian continent? So who are the ones that have carbon-datable sediment from the prehistoric soil of that continent gritting up their genes? The Tribals, the ones with pre-Hindu gods and goddesses? (The statement that Hinduism is the oldest religion in the world seems, now, a little wobbly.) What is my point of origin? How far back need I go to feel properly rooted? I must be looking for an Indian Cro-Magnon."

METANIL YELLOW K.
DADAJEE DHACKJEE & CO. PRIVATE LTD. EST'D 1894.

The orange powder floated up and entered Sushila's nostrils. She could taste its bitterness, feel it heavy in her lungs. She gave the deep orange jar a firm shake and about a teaspoon of the dye fell onto the smoothed mendhi mixture. Sushila took a hand cupped full of water and dribbled it over the dye. It turned deep reddish orange. She smeared it over the mendhi surface and watched it change from olive to orange brown. The colours were not her usual bright palette. They were the colours of the earth. She was deliriously transported in her imagination to the soils of her foreparents.

The tall Ismaili man behind the counter at Jamal Foods on Fraser Street had been suspicious when Sushila asked him for strong food colouring. "What do you want it for? You can't use it for food, you know. The Canadian government has prohibited its use in food. What do you want it for?" He held the orange jar in his hand and when she tried to hold it he pulled it back, pointing to the label for her to read:

NON EDIBLE

THE MATERIAL PACKED IN THIS PACKAGE IS EXCLUSIVELY FOR INDUSTRIAL USE FOR DYEING &/OR COLOURING PURPOSE AND AS SUCH EXEMPTED FROM PACKAGE COMMODITY RULE 1977.
VIDE RULE 34 CHAPTER V

She explained that she was not using it for food, but as a pigment for painting. And he said, yes, she can use it as a dye, but not in food, he was obliged to make that clear. Actually, he said, people always come to buy it for food colouring and he fulfills his obligation to say that it is banned as food, but he knows what they are really doing with it. After she paid for the mendhi and the metanil yellow K the man said, well you know, he was now nearly eighty years old and his mother has been using the metanil ever since he was a boy in Uganda, and nothing has happened to him yet. In fact when she asks him to bring home food colouring (yes she is still alive, almost a hundred years old and still making meethai, oh she is the best!) she insists that he bring metanil, and when he says that it is not good for them to use as food, she says, who says so? The Canadian government? What do they know about Indian sweets? Nothing! Those other colourings are useless. She has used it since she was a child. Bring only metanil. So he does, and look at him, he has never been ill a day since they arrived in Canada in '72.

"If you really are using it for painting you must wear gloves," he warned her. "You won't be able to get it out of your hands and nails for weeks. And don't get it on your clothes, it will never come out."

Sushila's hands were bright orange. There wasn't a hint of white or pink in her fingernails. The dye had trickled down her arm, marking a crooked trail to her elbow.

Images from her back-home filled her with yearning. Yearning for accurate details of Trinidad, the substance behind the visuals that left indelible burns on the retina of her memory. Hosay and Phagwa, one a Muslim festival, the other Hindu. The details and their significance were lost to her now, the two festivals blurring into one in her videographic memory. Throngs of people out in the streets, some wearing white T-shirts made whiter by vibrant splashes of coloured dye, buckets full of purple water being elat-edly flung (travelling and landing in the slow-motion ecstasy of her mind) among, against and over jubilant crowds feverishly dancing to the beat of tassa drums, and chanting in the streets. As she tried to unblur details, to sort out which festival is which, the act of forgetting and remembering and inventing reminded her of her grandmother, who, like so many other Trinidadian Hindus and Muslims she knows, refused to eat either beef or pork because she couldn't remember which one it is that she, as a goodBrahminwoman, wasn't supposed to eat.

The mixture of mendhi and plaster was so thick and inviting that Sushila made fingerprints deep in it. She etched decorative squiggles and patterns and borders over the surface, the cavities and grooves filling up with the orange food colouring. She stood back and watched her painting. It was becoming more full of who she is. She was beginning to recognize in the painting, in herself, an identity being excavated. She played and fretted and worked and invented until she came to a junction where she could take a turn that skirted needing to be pinned down as

Hindu, or as "Indian," or as Trinidadian (in themselves difficult identities to pin down) in favour of attempting to write a story of her own, using her own tools. There were brief moments, brief but empowering, when she felt one with her past. Fleeting. Like a teasing window that opened a crack and instantly closed. But she has become adept at grasping the glimpses, like a hand skilfully snatching flies out of the air. And her delight was transparent. Her finger and hand imprints in the mendhi practically squealed with ecstasy.

The Bright New Year's Eve Night

I. BOBBY

Tanya sat as far away as she could, leaning against her door. Despondently, she stared out her window at nothing in particular for the entire drive to the restaurant.

The long angry silences between her and Bobby thickened the air in the car. The air itself had become tingly, as if she were being pricked by thousands of needles. This kind of silence was as frightening as a face inches away from hers and a hand wrapped around her throat threatening to squeeze tighter.

Go ahead. Ignore me, bitch! This is what happens when you take hours to get ready! We'd have been parked and eating by now if you didn't take so long with everything you do. Instead you've got me driving circles looking for a stupid parking space.

The words didn't need to be spoken for Tanya to know what was curdling in his brain. She spent quite a bit of time there — in his brain — anticipating his moves, an instinctual measure for survival. She could hardly breathe; she looked as if she were being stifled.

Oh yeah, giving me the silent treatment — so what's new about that, huh? Oh, woman, you just piss me off when you pretend to ignore me!

68

I know bloody well that you are aware of everything I'm doing right now. So why this little game, eh?

Look ... it's not just my fault. And it's not as if I am not trying, for God's sake! I take you out to my favourite restaurant for a nice dinner and a bit of fun and you won't even show a little appreciation. So damn sour all the time.

What the hell does she want out of me? She expects me to stay at home and lie in bed with her reading those stupid romance stories that I find under the pillow, under cushions, everywhere I turn? Or look at the frigging TV from morning till night?

What happened to the chick who wanted me to take her out into the world to experience everything? That's the one I fell in love with. Not this. You used to be so much fun when you were just an innocent kid. Now look at you. I can't read a damn thing on your stone-cold face.

That's what I get for taking you out of your miserable little hole. I put some decent clothes on you. Stuff you could never afford if it weren't for me. All that stuff you used to moan over and wish for from that stack of useless magazines piling up by your bedside. I got it all for you, gave you everything money could buy. But nowadays you're too fucking full of yourself! I put a little class in your life, honey, and don't you forget that! I did it!

Like a dragon protective of its existence, or on the scent of prey, he breathed long and heavy and hot. He gritted his teeth tightly against each other and gripped the steering wheel hard. The muscles in his neck cramped up.

The driver in a shiny red hatchback in front of them was chatting away, gesticulating wildly and laughing with her passenger, totally oblivious to his presence behind. She was crawling, as if he didn't exist. He blurted out with characteristic exasperation, "What the hell is going on with that dame?" and flashed his high beam erratically to signal his impatience. There was no response from Tanya, as if she were unconcerned about how late they were. Or as if she hadn't noticed that his silence was meaningful.

This relationship is just fucking stifling me. It could kill me! I should've listened to Tony and the others and got out a long time ago. It's so damn embarrassing how controlling of me she is around them. She had better behave herself tonight or else, New Year's Eve or no New Year's Eve, I'll give her something good and proper to suck lemon about.

Shit! What is wrong with me! I should have just got what I wanted and got the hell out of here before I got so tangled up with her.

This is so fucked…! Every time I decide to make a break I look at her face and I see how much she needs me. She'd be helpless on her own. I couldn't stand anyone else touching that face of hers. I'd rearrange theirs — and I'm not above fixing hers, too — if she started fooling around on me. Trouble is … I love her. She is mine. She belongs to me no matter what's going down between us.

Suddenly Bobby saw a parking space up ahead in the next aisle over. Since the woman in front of him was the only other driver in the parking lot, he thought he'd simply turn left and go up the aisle instead of going in a full circle following the "one direction only" arrows.

The woman driver ahead of him crawled along, yakking away to the passenger in her car. If only she would get out of the way, just move on up a little, he would be able to turn and get into the space. He pressed the horn a few times and growled, "Move it, move it, idiot."

Bobby turned to look at Tanya. She was deliberately avoiding him by staring out her window.

Impatiently he snapped, "Look … if you're going to be sour and sulking all night why didn't you just stay home?"

Whenever Bobby shouted, Tanya's body froze. There was always an uneasy edge, however, to the satisfaction this gave him. It made him feel a little old, a bit like his father. His voice softened, adding, "It's New Year's Eve."

And then, the futility of everything in his interaction with Tanya made him wildly frustrated, so much so that he banged his forehead with the palm of his hand and screamed, "Don't spoil it for me again, Tanya!"

Bobby turned his eyes back to the driver ahead but his full attention was on Tanya biting and ripping off the tip of one fingernail after another.

Trying to punish me, as if I triggered your sulking? Forget it, honey! I'm not taking the blame for any of this. Think again! Just you sit there and chew them off. Chew off every one of them! Don't expect me to jump. You know, the trouble with you is that I spoil you too much.

I treat you like nobody ever did before, bitch. I give you anything you want, don't I? Don't I? But you drive me to want to beat the shit out of you.

Just like my mother! Chomping on those nails, so you could hear her teeth clicking against them. Making as if she was so traumatized! A man could only put up with shit like that for so long. Poor Dad! No wonder the poor fellow ended up hitting Mom. It's simply out of frustration. Christ, I understand that! And, the thing is, she never learned. Always, always making him hit her like that!

In his mind he can see the dark purple, green and navy bruises on Tanya's shoulder blade. A curious satisfaction, pride of possession, comes over him when he watches them turn colour as

71

the days go by. He often has an intensely sexual desire to lick and suck on the bruises.

He hadn't meant to push her so hard the other day, but it was the third time that week that she scrambled his eggs too hard – and after he had taken the time to show her how to do them properly. She says that it's because she tries to have the toast, bacon, tea and eggs ready all at once, and it's hard to do all of that and have the eggs perfect. But to him it's almost as if she intends to anger him, purposely drying up the glisten just enough to bring on a fight. It's not as if he wasn't trying to curb his temper, but she doesn't make it easy for him!

The driver in front might as well have parked right there in the middle of the road. She hadn't moved more than a couple of centimetres in the last minute.

"What the hell is wrong with that broad? Drive that car, you moron."

And he lay his palm flat and heavy on the horn for several long seconds, still eyeing the parking space ahead. Suddenly the woman in front, as if responding to his impatience, took off with a screech, but instead of getting out of his way she swerved left up the one-way aisle, and landed in his parking stall. Bobby smacked the steering wheel with his fist. The veins in his neck and along his temples ripened. With exasperated, overemphasized movements he yanked the gear into neutral, pressed the button to wind down the window, and began shouting.

"Damn it, you idiot. That's illegal! You're not supposed to do that. Where the hell did you learn to drive? You can get a ticket for that – this is a public parking lot. You can't do that and get away with it."

Tanya put her hand on his lap to restrain him and urgently said, "What are you doing? Leave her alone, Bobby."

He leaned his head far out the window, waving his hand about in the cold air, shouting at the woman.

"What's your problem? You're not the only one on the road you know!"

"Whey yuh expect mih to do? It have a woman walking in front mih – yuh want mih to knock her down?"

"Use your brain, use your horn! And you could get a ticket for going in that direction, you know."

"Oh, go take a Valium, asshole. I was in front anyway!"

Bobby's car screeched off with attitude. Then he came to a sudden halt, parking the car illegally in the middle of the neighbouring lane. He got out and kicked the door shut with such force that the car rocked in shock.

2. TANYA

Tanya deliberately shunned him by staring out of her window, but she was aware of every move he made, every breath he took.

I wish he weren't so impatient. Oh Bobby, just calm down! Please! Can't you see there is someone walking in front of her car? I wish he'd just leave it alone.... We're not in any big rush; midnight is still hours away.

Bobby suddenly addressed her, snapping, shouting. He accused her of sulking and being "sour." She dared not utter a word to him when he was so edgy. She stifled her tears and bit on her lower lip until she tasted a bead of blood.

I want to scream. Or just cry. But I can't really say why. What's there to be happy about? So what if it's New Year's Eve?

I know the ending of all of this too well, first from Mama and Papa, and now I'm living the same hell. What do I go out with you for, only to be embarrassed by your drunkenness and you puking all over everything, ignoring me and flirting with every other woman, and threatening everybody. This is not the kind of New Year's Eve I dream about.

You should have let me stay at home like I wanted to. I just know you'll end up mad at me. I'll spoil your night. I could never understand why Mama would let Papa ruin every happy moment she saw coming, and now the same thing's happening to me.

I wish I could leave right now. If I could afford rent and hydro and groceries on my own, I would jump out of this car right this minute.

I'd be so scared and lonely on my own, though.

Sometimes when you hold me it's all I want in the world. I don't want your jewelry. I don't want any more itchy fancy dresses. I don't want any more stuff. Just hold me, Bobby, just protect me … I feel so exposed and empty.

God! Bobby, don't scream at me like that, please!

When Bobby screamed at her not to spoil his evening, the bruises on her shoulder came alive, aching and cramping up her entire shoulder blade. She dared not flinch for fear of setting him off. The muscles at the back of her neck, under her skull, were taut enough to be plucked like the strings of a musical instrument. Her forehead was throbbing uncontrollably. Methodically, she bit off one fingernail after another, concentrating on the taste of bittersweet hand-soap trapped underneath her nails.

I wish this pounding in my head would stop.

I can't seem to do anything right, Bobby. I know that I make you mad at every little thing I do. But you can't even ... you can't even let me ... something as simple as ... hum a tune, in peace. It's not really such a big deal if I can't carry one, is it? In any case, nobody ever told me that before. You make me feel awful when you turn on the radio every time I begin to sing.

God, this pounding in my temples is awful. I could tear my hair out.

What on earth makes him so impatient? But if I point out the woman walking in front of the car ahead he might just chew my head off.

Thank heavens (still, I am shocked ...) that he didn't get angry about the way I pressed his shirt tonight. I really hurried, tried to do everything right, didn't want to keep him waiting. I don't think I can stand being hit again right now. And yet part of me, some distant part, wants him to get real physical so that I can just tear at him, like that woman on the TV show the other day – was she ever brave! The man had been following her around and tried to rape her once and she got away from him without any damage done to her, but when she reported the incident to the police they said that there was not enough evidence to open a file. And then he got into her house one night and waited for her to come home. He tried to rape her again and he tore at her clothing and hit her over and over so that she fell and got huge bloody gashes across her face and arms and legs. But she fought back like an enraged animal and managed to grab a fire stoker and whip it across his chest. When he fell she tore the skin off his face with one clean scrape of all her fingernails, and then she tied him up and stuffed him in the fireplace. I'm a little ashamed at how gleefully I was cheering her on while she just about killed a man, but I'd never before seen a woman defend herself like that on TV – and the rapist got what he deserved. Not jail, but a good near-death bludgeoning from his victim! But that's TV and anything is possible there.

*I wonder if I could possibly ever fight back like that. I **can** picture how to do it – goodness! I think about it often enough, especially when I'm cleaning my own blood off my mouth and nose. It sure was good to see a woman do it – even though it was just TV.*

But the reality is that every time we fight, even before he hits me I get so weak and tired and sleepy. No energy to even lift my arm.

My shoulder hurts so bad. This is how Mama's head must have felt every time Papa banged it into the wall.

If Bobby hits me one more time ... I don't want to survive it. In fact, I hope to God that he does hit me so hard next time that I fall and hit my head. That'll serve him right! I'll never get back up again.

Never think again. Never feel again.

When the driver ahead was clear of the pedestrian, she sped up, turned left, and parked in an empty stall. Bobby began shouting out his window at the woman and hitting the steering wheel with his fist, reacting as if he had been personally attacked.

Goodness! She got him! She got him good! Oh God! He's going to hate this one! I should be frightened but I just want to laugh like crazy. I can feel my cheeks beginning to crack up in a smile. This is the first moment all day that I have felt like bursting out laughing. But he better not catch me loving this.

Although she was able to preserve the glumness and sullenness around her mouth, a lightness came over her for a brief and precious moment.

The woman driver nonchalantly threw out "Oh, go take a Valium, asshole" to Bobby over her shoulder. Bobby took off with a screech, then a couple of seconds later he braked to a halt, again with a hair-raising screech. Tanya reached her hand across, grabbed his leg and snapped uncharacteristically, "Bobby! Come back here. Leave her alone! Stop it, Bobby!"

But it was too late. He flung her hand roughly off his leg and left the car, slamming the door behind him. The car trembled for a good few seconds in the middle of the road where he left it. Tanya fumbled nervously to get out, even though she knew that nothing that she could do would hold him back. From where she stood behind the car she saw his stocky muscular body lunging with gale force toward the other car. She saw him wedge his large frame full and square in the driver's open doorway. She didn't notice how cold her hands were, or that she was shivering with fear. She bit the remainder of her nails....

3. RANI AND MEENA

When the man in the car behind pressed his horn long and hard Rani didn't look at him in her rear-view mirror. This time she turned her body around and glared at him through the rear windshield. Meena also turned and frowned and shook her head at him. Rani said, "But dat man doh have no patience or what! He only flashin-flashin up his lights and now what he makin so much noise for?"

And she sucked her teeth in a long drawn-out cheups. Meena, more concerned about why people do things than merely irritated by what they do, commented, "He must be in a hurry, nah." Which annoyed Rani further.

"Yes but is not as if I takin mih cool time. If I go any faster I go hit de woman. What she think she doing, anyway, walking in de middle of de road, slow slow like she own it? Humph!"

They turned around to face the front and continued inching

77

ahead. Meena thought it best to distract Rani from sliding into one of her little tirades about the frustrations of being a driver.

"So yes, you were saying?" And they resumed their previous conversation.

"Listen nah, Meena, I tellin yuh all dis in strictest confidence, yuh understand, yuh mustn't say I say so, yuh hear, girl!"

"Yes, yes, who yuh think I have in dis country to blag with but you? Hurry up and carry on."

"I see she with mih own two eyes! And it was de same fella yuh describing just now. De same yellow hair and blue eyes. Well, child! He good lookin fuh so!"

"Yuh think so too, eh! He is a real good looker, fuh true. He look like he come straight out from de TV set!"

"But, Meenagirl, dem fellas only like we kind a women because dey does see we like we some tropical fancy bird decorating dey surroundings for dem. *And!* dey *think* dey could control we!"

Meena agreed reluctantly ("Eh heh"), not quite wanting to believe that such good-looking men could be so misguided.

Rani took her hand off the steering wheel and put it on her waist, akimbo, and opened her eyes very widely, staring at the woman who was walking directly in the centre of the road and making no effort to get out of the way.

"Look! Ah gettin vex now! What happen to dis woman, she jes takin she cool time, oui!"

"Doh blow yuh horn at she, nah! Suppose now yuh blow it and she get frighten and get heart attack! So carry on, nah girl, ah waitin to hear more."

"Well, I doin mih Christmas shoppin, and I see de two a dem in de line-up by de cash register, and he only rubbing he hand up and down she back like if he burping she."

"And poor Ralphie, he must be doh suspect a thing."

"Nothing, child! Just day-before I eat dinner by dem and poor Ralphie look like he doh have a inkling whatsoever."

"So what happen in de grocery? She see yuh?"

"When she see mih she pull away from him and makin like she doh know him, and he stand up looking baffle like hell."

Suddenly the driver at the back started banging on his horn and ended the string of angry staccato beeps with one long blaring one. Right then Rani spotted an empty stall and swung her car sharply left up the one-way aisle (going in the wrong direction) and pulled into the space.

Rani opened her car door to get out but Meena wanted to hear the whole story without any more interruptions, so she insisted that they sit right there until Rani had told her everything. The driver who had been behind them stopped his car and was shouting something at them. It was a couple of seconds before Rani realized that he was shouting at her. Not intending to be confrontational, Rani threw her response carelessly over her shoulder, "Whey yuh expect mih to do? It have a woman walking in front mih – yuh want me to knock her down?"

"Use your brain, use your horn! And you could get a ticket for going in that direction, you know."

Pointing out even a single one of Rani's many harmless illegalities was certainly a mistake. Her fearless temper reared up and she tersely spat her words straight at his face.

"Oh, go take a Valium, asshole. I was in front anyway!"

He said nothing more but there was a loud screech as he took off. Meena never got to hear the rest of her story. Rani, furiously agitated, went on and on about what an abrasive idiot that man was. In fact, she had become so distracted by his petty accusation that she did her characteristic withdrawal into anger. She furiously pulled out a little black plastic bottle from the pocket of her car door, squeezed a firm shot of interior wax onto the dash, and with more force than necessary, began obsessively scrubbing and polishing.

Meena sat quietly wondering about the ethics of going in the wrong direction to get to a parking space that would have been theirs anyway, since there was no one ahead of them. Suddenly she saw the driver walking towards them on Rani's side of the car.

"Rani, Rani. Look! He comin!"

Rani said, "Who?" and carried on quarrelling about how people in this country are always in such a hurry, just don't know how to relax and take it easy. Not until he had wedged himself in the opening of the door and blocked the beam of the streetlight on the dashboard did Rani look up to see his black-suited, bow-tied torso, and two clenched fists at his side.

Meena felt her heart leap into her mouth and her brain become quite confused. She scanned the car to see if there was something weapon-like that she could wield if necessary. Not finding anything in the car but a box of tissues, she looked outside for people walking about in the parking lot. There was no one, except one woman standing, almost hiding, behind a car that was parked right in the middle of the neighbouring lane. Meena wondered if it was the same car that the man had been driving. It was hard to tell in the night light.

Rani had turned and seemed to be touching the man's arm, brushing against him so that she could get out of the car. For a moment Meena was not sure what was happening.

She opened her door and got out just in time to hear the man say, "I didn't touch you, woman. You touched me first."

"You're in my space. Move!" Rani answered fiercely.

She again touched the man's shoulder, this time actually pushing him. Suddenly it became quite clear to Meena that the man was trying to pick a fight. He said menacingly, quietly, "And that wasn't very nice, calling me 'asshole.'"

Without thinking Meena craned her neck over the top of the car roof and began screaming at the man, who had ignored her until then.

"Back off! Back off of her!"

The man looked over and raised one hand to his inside jacket pocket. Meena screamed, "Get away from de car, get away!"

She stopped screaming when she saw Rani move the man aside with her arm and say to him with a tone of incredulous ridicule, "So? Is dat supposed to scare me?"

Appearing unshaken, but actually brazened by her outrage, Rani shut the car door and briskly walked past the man toward the trunk. The man turned to face Meena, who found herself walking straight toward him, shaking with fear but heading straight at him. He stuck his chest out at her, and said, "Who was talking to you anyway? Mind your own business."

Rani locked the trunk and without looking at him said to Meena, "Leave him. You know where his brain is."

The man suddenly turned and walked slowly away. In a voice so loud that it curdled the bright New Year's Eve night, Meena shouted out at his back, "*Asshole!*"

4. JUST ANOTHER NIGHT

Tanya limply dialled a number and waited a brief moment. Staring out the window, her eyes landing aimlessly in the vicinity of the snow-capped bush on the ragged patch of front yard, she quietly and without emotion stated her case into the mouthpiece.

"I think my boyfriend is dead. I think I just killed him."

She managed to put the receiver back in its cradle. Without glancing down at the large body sprawled around the legs of the kitchen table, the head in a halo of blood, she walked around it, out into the hallway and to the front door. She unlocked the door for them, turned off the lights, and entered the dark living room on the other side of the hallway. Feeling like a stranger in the house that she had lived in for the last eighteen months, she sat in the armchair that was neither his nor hers but reserved for guests. Her hands began to shake first, then her shoulders and chest, then her teeth chattered loudly against each other, either with fright or with cold, maybe both, and she patiently waited.

Seconds later she heard distant sirens, first one, then two, then several whining, getting louder and more urgent as they came closer. It occurred to her that whenever she heard a cop car flying past the house she would distractedly think in passing, someone's done something ... somebody got hurt....

She thought to herself that this time the sirens would come to a halt outside Bobby's house and the neighbours would all look out their windows and cautiously spill onto the far sidewalk, curious. The police might even have been called by one of them, she thought; the shouting and screaming had been loud and long enough.

Several cars screeched to a halt. It sounded as if one might have mounted the pavement and landed in the front yard. The sirens had stopped abruptly.

Red and blue lights winged rhythmically across the living room window, lighting up the room and her face each time they whizzed by.

From far off, as if from one of her favourite television programs turned down low, a man's voice yelled to the occupants to come out, to show themselves, to drop their weapons. The voice filtered through a megaphone, sounding tinny. From the armchair Tanya could see the beams from flashlights reaching across the kitchen to the hallway, obviously coming through the kitchen window. There, they would have seen Bobby's body on the floor. They banged at the kitchen door and shouted for it to be opened.

She heard the front door being hesitantly opened. It dragged, scraped heavily along the floor at the opening. She had suggested to Bobby only the day before to lift the fallen hinges and set the door in the jamb properly. She'd seen a man do it on a home improvement show.

The instant they entered they saw her sitting, waiting in the dark, engulfed by a too-large armchair, the room lit only by the swift rhythm of the red and blue spinning lights from the cars outside. Four of the men swung toward her with their arms extended, guns cocked and aimed, their legs spread and bodies lowered at the knees. They bounced from one spot to the next, as if expecting her to pounce, until they all surrounded her. She remained still, a disinterested blankness in her wary stare. One cop slowly made his way around to face her. He cautiously lowered himself in front of her until his eyes held hers. Without blinking, he whispered, "Just don't move. Don't move. It's over now. It's all over."

The red and blue lights whirled hypnotically across Tanya's face, mingling with several new bruises smudged along her cheeks and temples to create an eerie mask that made her look much older than nineteen.

Already a crowd of men in different uniforms was taking over the kitchen. Without a fuss, she let herself be escorted outside.

She left through the front door without a glance toward the kitchen floor.

Last Day Pandemonium and Heart Beats

My first "last day" in high school. Last day of the term before Christmas holidays.

Assembly this morning was brief. It began formal and restrained as usual, heads bowed, hands at our sides.

Mother Superior wished us a safe and holy holiday, and urged us to keep Christ in Christmas, and to remember the poor and homeless. Parbatee Gopaul, Mother Elena's favourite piano student, accompanied Maria Gonzales-Samuel, who is the pride of our school for all the acclaim and medals she has won us and herself at The National Annual Conservatory of Music festival. She sang "O Holy Night," solo.

After assembly Mother dismissed us with her usual, "You may go to your classrooms now, and remember to act with the decorum expected of young ladies!" This morning she added, "Especially since you have no formal classes today." Instead of our usual school-day structure, all that was scheduled was the classroom clean-up and our Christmas concert, for which many students had been rehearsing for the last few weeks, even, in some cases, during the end-of-term exams. Normally, after she has dismissed us, we must wait until she leaves the podium before our Head Girl signals us to begin walking off to our rooms, line by line, form by form. But this morning before the Head Girl could signal us, the expected decorum disintegrated, crumbled without warning. Last-day-of-school excitement erupted, and straight lines to the classrooms unravelled. The Form Ones didn't dare break the lines, though; we have been warned enough about not engaging the wrath of Mother Superior. But the girls from the higher forms broke their line-ups-by-class and crossed over to friends in other classes to exchange presents, hug and kiss good-bye, and enquire after any post-exam news.

Lack of our familiar regimen made it easy to break away into pandemonium uncharacteristic of an early morning assembly in a convent. From above I could just imagine what we might have looked like! An ant nest, I am sure, whose regimented life had suddenly been disturbed, the ants crazily scurrying off in all directions. Wild twittering soon became excited talking, then shouting, and as the din grew louder and it became impossible for us to hear even ourselves (we Form Ones had by this time joined in the mêlée), the shouting became competitive. The House prefects, honour students from the senior forms, looked distraught as they ran amongst our lineless mob snapping, "Get into your lines," punctuated by a forefinger pressed to their lips, forcing "shhhs" out between their teeth. They threatened to give out "marks," abandoning "dots" altogether.

I myself have never been given either a dot or a mark, and I do tread carefully to avoid receiving either. Dots are bad points, quick to be given for talking when one is not supposed to, or for long fingernails, or for dirty sneakers or an unpressed skirt. Three dots equal one bad mark. However, one can easily rack up straight marks for rudeness, for wearing nail polish, or for talking to boys outside the school gates. Some prefects have been known to become so irate in the face of an unrepentant student that they would open their mark book and press the pencil into the page so hard that the paper would rip, or the pencil's point would break off, and then they would further humiliate and insult the student/victim by having to borrow her pencil to complete the record.

A certain prefect, angered that she has not been able to force a certain stone to bleed, has been known to dig her pencil into the page of her mark book and begin a furious up and down etching to create one mark expressive of her own frustration with this particular student. Or, the said prefect may begin slamming mark after mark onto the page. One could end up in her book with ten marks for the same offence. The House mistresses, however, are all aware that while this prefect is an "eagle eye" and can spot an undesirable thought that has not yet left the mind of a student, she does indeed have a low tolerance for rule breakers. House mistresses accommodate her by counting her numerous marks against a student as a single mark, and Eagle Eye's desire to give multiple marks is appeased by sentencing the offender to a week of after-school detentions. But after the penance is carried out there is still the never thoroughly appeased wrath of that same prefect to deal with for the rest of one's life.

The threat, however, of getting a mark on the last day of school, when we felt as if there were no future school term, held no sway over most of us today. So excited and unrestrained was the noise that it sounded like break-time, not the beginning of our school day.

The microphone in the courtyard had already been turned off after assembly. From speakers on the roof-top corners at the periphery of the courtyard came loud crackling as the microphone was again switched on. It produced a loud electronic shriek, which brought us to attention. Most of us, that is. The volume of the microphone was adjusted and the stern, firm, un-Christmasy voice of Mother Superior boomed over the system.

"Young ladies!" And louder yet, "Young ladies! What nonsense is this?" She was almost squealing, as if she were caught by the lid of a desk. We looked over to the assembly podium but only a feeble old nun who is not a teacher looked out at us, helpless and stunned by this unruly mob of young ladies. Necks and heads began stretching upward, everyone on tiptoes searching over a sea of heads for Mother Superior. She sounded fifteen feet tall. Eventually I saw her, a tiny head, body down to her waist peeping out of the staff room window, one hand holding the microphone and the other's index finger wagging in front of the crucifix that rests prominently on her breast.

"School has not as yet ended. I have never before in my entire life as a teacher in a convent for young ladies heard such raucous behaviour. You sound like a bunch of fishwives. Get back into your lines. I do not want to hear a sound from any one of you. You will stand out here in absolute silence until I tell you to move."

Then she screeched. Her high-pitched scream rang through the courtyard, ricocheting off the walls of the buildings like a billiard ball hit with wild force.

"Miss Clarke, I will not tolerate such insolence! Get into my office right now! The rest of you will stand here until I am satisfied that you know the meaning of silence."

Mother Superior disappeared from the window and seconds later could be seen in the courtyard charging towards Nadine Clarke, the Form Three troublemaker, boy-crazy wearer of nail polish and eye make-up, who was sauntering casually to the office. They met and squared off. Mother's body leaned into Nadine. I could see them but I could not hear their conversation. Mother's head bobbed and her finger wagged.

Nadine stared blankly, the eyes of a dead fish mesmerized by the dance of the muscles around Mother's mouth as she formed her words, designed to elicit a burning-at-the-stake effect. Nadine's eyes rolled off as if involuntarily, and caught on the crucifix on Mother's chest. With immense effort they floated back up to rest on a large fleshy wine-coloured mole on Mother's right cheek. After a few minutes of scolding, Mother walked behind Nadine and gave her a firm shove in the direction of the principal's office. Then she began casing the lines, searching out insolents, to assuage a sudden hunger. The rest of us froze, not daring even to turn our heads.

The sun was beginning to move over the courtyard, and as the shade receded, the heat made a noticeable contrast. Sweat beads, strung together, sat on my chest, my underarms became slippery, and there were ticklish trickles running down a canal in the centre of my back. My undershirt stuck to my skin. Occasionally a thin breeze would blow and I would unstick my arms from my sides to catch the wind in the sleeve of my shirt and allow it to bellow up under my arms.

Memories of making trips with my mother and the servant to the downtown abattoir and fish market, before it was torn down for health reasons, came rushing back to me. I would trail behind, linked to my mother, at arm's length, by a hooked finger. Drinking in smells and colours and sounds. Raw blood from freshly slaughtered goats, pigs, cows, chickens, as it tumbled down the open drains, searing itself into the lining of my nose. Pink, glistening carcasses of dead animals hanging just above my head, casting an iridescent blue sheen as they swung on their ropes.

And the seafood section. Stale pungency of the previous week's, the previous month's, the previous year's catch rides high over this area. The trays that hold fresh live conches breathe, almost swaying. Blue sea crabs that struggle against tight green twines that bind their legs and claws, the odd one here and there waving an escaped, menacing gundy. Pink-bodied shrimp, large and slightly curved with heavy grey armour over their heads. Pale grey baby shrimp, translucent except for a fine thread of greeny black down their backs. And fish. Manta rays, bluish-brown-grey, eyes on their backs. Huge crayfish. Brown lobsters. Charcoal grey scaleless shark, rows of fine, sharp white teeth biting together. Glistening silver carite. Redfish. Flying fish. Moonfish. Sounds of people calling out what they want, complaining of high prices, asking after people they haven't seen in a while. And the sound of the fishwives. Business-like yet excited, competing yet jovial voices asking whether to scale and clean, to slice into steaks, or to fillet. "You want the head for soup? We get in fresh snapper, good for stuffing and baking, mightn't get for a long time again. Best price 'specially for you today. Want some today darling?" The language of the market, lilting, necessarily loud, joking, friendly, warm. *You sound like a bunch of fishwives.* I failed to see the insult Mother Superior intended.

The school grounds were soundless now. One could hear the proverbial pin drop. Even the teachers tiptoed around the school halls at the edges of the courtyard.

It seemed as if we had been standing still for an eternity but actually only ten minutes passed before the gentler voice of Mother Anthony, the vice-principal, came over the PA system. She was talking from the staff room, looking out at us from the window there.

"Good morning, children. Today, as you know, there will be no formal classes. I trust that everyone has brought ample rags and a jar of soapy water. As soon as you get to your classrooms, your form mistresses will oversee the cleaning of the desks, the blackboards and the floors. Please do not leave any of your belongings on the school premises. If anything is left behind it will find its way to the garbage by tomorrow morning. We are not a caretaking facility, you know!"

She smiled. Most of us smiled. The glacier was melting. But not knowing the whereabouts of Mother Superior, from which corner she was eyeing us, we remained cautiously demure.

"Clean-up will end at ten o'clock. Then there will be a half-hour break. When the bell rings we will line up in forms and enter the auditorium for our Christmas concert, where we will all act like good, happy young ladies, I am sure. Now girls, quietly walk to your classrooms. Form One move off first."

When we moved off, all that could be heard was the shuffle of feet. Gradually, a whisper here and a whisper there were braved.

During clean-up we competed with each other to see who could restore her desk to the most new-looking condition. Years of grime accumulated against half-hearted efforts at end-of-term clean-ups came off in my jar of soapy water, fast rendering it useless. Grime in grooves unwedged itself to reveal incised messages, territorial markings, expletives and comments about subjects, teachers and boys. I almost wished that I had not cleaned so well as to leave exposed a certain four-letter expletive gouged in clear one-inch letters on the lid of my desk. During break-time I would use the point of my compass to gouge fresh lines and scratch out others to transform the expletive to the less offensive word "fool."

By the time everything was cleaned – all the desks, including Miss Small's, the blackboard and the inside of the windows – we still had about half an hour before we could leave the classroom for "break." We sat back in our damp desks waiting for the bell to ring. Some girls, terrified at the idea of suffering the same fate as Nadine Clarke, whatever it was, and ears still ringing and skin burning from Mother Superior's barrage, took out books and quietly read. Some went up to Miss Small's desk and clung to her chair, her arms and the desk, asking what she would be doing for the Christmas holidays, a preamble to did she already know who came first in this subject or that, and who came first overall. But she wasn't born yesterday, as she kept reminding them, all the while laughing good-naturedly. She could see right through us children, and was not revealing any end-of-term results.

She said that she had to go and finish marking exam papers but would send a school prefect to stay with us until the bell rang. I hoped that it wouldn't be Eagle Eye. When she left, Althea Ferguson, affectionately – perhaps also jealously? – called "Brainsome," from Form Six, came and sat at the desk. Once again the same students went up to her, asking which university she was hoping to go to and what did she want to become when she grew up. Althea Ferguson had recently won the national gold medal at O levels and, even though she had gone into liberal arts at A levels, any student with ambition wanted to be just like her.

Sitting back at my own desk, not really doing anything more than observing the goings-on around me, I happened to glance out the window and saw Miss Small and Mrs. Mohansingh scurrying out the school gates like puppies that had just stolen a cooked chicken. I wasn't about to squeal on them but a few other children saw them and pointed them out, saying with the excitement of being in the know, "Ay! All yuh look! She ain't marking papers, nah! They gone Christmas shopping. Look, all yuh, look! Bu' A A!"

I have never had the nerve to go and talk with Althea. She is a lot older than I, about five years older, and taller. She is also white, and she walks with her shoulders upright, confidently. I am shy to be caught watching her. When she won her gold medal she was interviewed on television, where she talked about her favourite subject, English literature, and she listed off her favourite books and authors. In the last few weeks I've borrowed and read three of the books she named: *The Hobbit, Great Expectations*, and *Grapes Of Wrath*.

Radha Ramkissoon, a classmate, made a sketch on the blackboard of a beach scene with coconut trees and a black Santa playing the steel pan. She turned and asked Althea to finish colouring it. Althea called out to me to do it, saying that she had heard that I could do a much better job than anyone else. My heart skipped a beat and when it kicked back in it began racing and I became wide-eyed. Thankfully, yet sadly, the school bell rang.

The girls jumped up without waiting for Althea to dismiss us, and burst out of the classroom. The same rupture was happening throughout the school. I wish I could have shown Althea my skill, but the thought of standing at the blackboard in front of her with my stooped shoulders and chubby body made my cheeks burn. On the other hand, I was thrilled to the point of being squeaky-voiced (inside my own head) that not only did she know of my existence, but my reputation as the best art student in our class had filtered all the way up to Form Six, and to her. For a few brief seconds my shoulders straightened and I stayed back inside the classroom by myself, grinning widely. Even now, just thinking about it, I still have what you might call a silly smile right across my face.

Nocturnals

I cannot get to sleep at night without being plagued by the thought of my mother growing older in another country. I have neglected (for no reason other than the busy-ness of my life) to see her for eight years. Not long ago when I received a photograph of her and my father taken on their fortieth wedding anniversary I thought, for one confusing moment, that I had been sent a photo of my maternal grandmother, who has been deceased for many years, and my father. My mother's head was entirely grey. Before I left she had only ever let herself be seen with two or three strands of very dark brown hair whitening at their roots. She would ask one of us to pluck them for her and then she'd rush off to the hairdresser's to have her entire head coloured very dark brown, almost black, except for when light would shine on it, bringing out the red in the black.

I always mean to see her soon. My friends tell me that I must be waiting for an emergency to justify stopping work. I noticed in the photograph that her once thin-skinned tight cheeks now hang slightly on either side of her jaws. I can't get to sleep at night without thinking of her, and I never unplug my phone at night even though I prefer nightmares to middle-of-the-night telephone calls.

I.

Although I have never even been pregnant, I dreamt, last night, that I gave birth.

Before I knew it a little baby lay on my chest. I reached to snip off its lifeline. It had somehow already been severed. The afterbirth was absent, swallowed up inside me; I could feel it tumbling around in me. The baby lay on me immobile and I remembered hearing something about slapping a newborn's bum to induce life. I tapped it lightly so as not to hurt its soft fair skin, but the child remained lifeless. Stillborn? I thought, no way! Not after I carried it in me for so long, even though I never even knew I was pregnant.

I tapped harder and its face set up to cry but still no sound came, and in a panic, knowing it must breathe quickly, I slapped it three times but not too hard, and it cried, and so did I, in happiness. The prettiest little baby I ever saw, and then I remembered to check its gender, anticipating, hoping for a girl child. But there between its legs was its perfectly defined and autonomous boy-thing, and I was disappointed. I looked again to see if I could make it into a girl, but it remained as before. I looked up to its face and it was still the prettiest baby you ever saw.

So I ran to tell my parents. One foot ran toward them with the joy of this little human, even if it were a boy, and the other ran toward them to show that I had fulfilled my duty as a woman and they could now be proud of me. And the first thing they said was, "How will this child grow up without a father?" The little boy child, taller and bigger than a newborn baby, ran about in the garden naked and free. My sisters and their husbands clasped their own children to their chests.

2.

Last night I dreamt that my sisters, brother and mother headed from overseas to my grandparents' house in England by car (you know how accommodating dreams can be). I made my way there, also by car, from Canada. Together we made a bee-line for the city of London, arriving simultaneously. My own arrival went unnoticed.

In the area just outside London, not a vehicle or person was in sight, not a wind stirred. Peering through windows of empty businesses and houses along our route revealed to me that an evacuation had recently taken place. Picket-fence gates around homes were left wide open, as if abandoned in haste. The city was deserted.

The rest of my family, entirely unperturbed by the urgency in London's stillness, were obsessively intent on eating immediately at one of London's famous Indian restaurants. The only one among us aware of any danger was myself, but my family seemed not to have noticed that I was with them. "Something's wrong. Look! There is a problem in this city. We must get out of here right away. Let's go now!" I begged, but they did not hear the words I was shouting to them. My brother poured through the Michelin guide to restaurants and the others kept their eyes peeled on the desolation for a flashing neon sign, an open door.

Soon we came to a shrimp-pink building with a shrimp-pink staircase that led upstairs to an open door. A Thai restaurant. That would do – they were quite famished by then. We clambered all the way up and entered. The dining room was being emptied of the last shrimp-pink chair through the back door. A scent of Thai basil and lemon grass hung in the air. A small group of men and women dressed in the same shrimp pink knelt

96

one behind the other in Buddhist prayer. The oldest man turned toward us and said, "We are closed, I am very sorry. We remained open as long as we could but we must evacuate now. You should go home. Please go now."

I tugged at my family to head immediately for my grandparents' house, and we did, but not because of the danger that was tangible to me; they had merely become bored with the dampness of London's welcome and were ready to settle down for the rest of the day.

Through the kitchen window of my grandparents' house I could see the back yard and beyond, red-dotted apple trees and lush pear trees, a homemade swing dangling from one of the trees, garden sheds, tools and tubs of clothing abandoned in the middle of a busy day. Suddenly a sound like the crumpling of brown paper, magnified a thousand times, drew my eyes through the thick foliage in the back yard to the horizon. A cloud of thick grey dust, or maybe smoke, in the distance was rapidly rising over the business section of London. The crumpling continued and gusts of heavy grey puffed upwards into the sky. The city was clearly under an attack of some sort.

Instinctively I rushed out to the back yard, shouting for my mother to get out of the house at once. Wireless radios in every house on the street crackled and the voice of an announcer boomed across the yards and echoed onto the streets. "The city of London is under siege. I repeat, London is under attack. Those of you who have not evacuated, do not, I repeat, do not stay in your houses. Please remain calm and make your way to your back yards or to the streets, well away from buildings. Leave your houses at once. Leave your houses at once. Lie close to the ground. London is under attack."

My sisters, brother and mother ran out of the house into the back yard. A large shadow from the fine dust which filled the air fell over the city. Two of my sisters stood huddled in the middle of the back yard. My mother and brother raced down to hide behind a galvanized fence that I had crouched next to. My mother pulled him close to her, tucked him into her chest. I saw my grandparents still in the house, standing motionless together, peering blankly out of their kitchen window at the obliterated horizon. I screamed at them to get out of the house. They slowly took one step back from the window and remained there staring out into the distance. Explosions were now audible and crawling in our direction.

We looked upwards to where a high-pitched slow whizzing arched across the laden sky. It came from a ball of blinding silver light that was fizzing out high up in the sky. I screamed, "Get down, get down on the ground." Beneath the ball, not far away from us, the earth erupted and the ground we hugged convulsed with the thundering. My brother pulled himself out of my mother's clutch, got up and ran over to my sisters to join their huddle. Fearfully she shouted after him. To comfort myself and my mother I stretched out a hand and wrapped it around her ankle. She stared blankly at my hand, and then with hopeless terror in her eyes she looked over to her other children. I wondered if her terror was because of the bombing or because my hand was holding onto her ankle.

The sound of my roommate opening and shutting her door awakened me. My heart was thumping ferociously and my legs tingled, numbed with fright. They were too weak to budge. From my waist down I felt paralyzed. I closed and opened my hands for assurance. A gleaming new sun poured through the window, spotlighting a shaft of lazily dancing dust that for the briefest moment resembled ascending clouds of sediment from crumbling buildings. The morning traffic thundering heavily on the street below my apartment had already built up and become impatient with itself.

3.

The telephone rings, ripping me panting from the heart of my sleep. My heart is thumping so loudly that it seems to have drowned out the phone. The ringing seems to have receded, now, way back, as if it were part of my dream. I lie dead still waiting for a ring. The digital clock by my bed blares fluorescent red, 2:12 A.M. There it is: another mournful ring, and now the ringing seems to have been going on long before I was awakened by it. Without another second's hesitation I leap over clothing strewn on my bedroom floor to grab the phone before the caller hangs up.

Just in case the electricity might have screwed up the clock in my bedroom I check the time on the battery-run wall-clock in the dark living room. The instant my hand touches the receiver my legs become weak.

"Hello?" My voice is sharp – ready for business – ready to handle any situation.

"Hello, Sonita?" On the mere breath of the "h" in hello I recognize the sound of my mother's voice. "It's Mummy. Are you awake?"

Relief. It's her, so my worst fear is not yet about to come true. I picture my mother not as she appeared in the photograph of her and my father that was recently sent to me but as I remember her before I left. I remain cautious ... something serious must surely have happened. My mind, yanked out of sleep too sharply, races crazily, trying to anticipate so as to have more than a shred of control. This something that must have happened would likely not be to my brother or sisters. My mother would never be able to phone me herself if something had happened to any of her other children. She would be uncontrollable. To my father perhaps. She might be calmer if it were about him. Perhaps she has decided to leave him and needs to talk.

"It's okay, Mummy. I was sleeping, but it's okay."

"What time is it there?"

"It's two-fifteen."

"Oh! It's four here. I always forget … you are two hours behind, not ahead." But what are you doing awake and phoning me at this time of your pitch-black night, anyway? my mind races. I know that she and my father have bitter disagreements, fights, to be frank, and she sometimes gets depressed enough to seriously consider killing herself.

"It's alright, Mummy. Is something…?" I can't ask.

"Sonita? Listen. Something terrible has happened. Something awful." My heart begins thundering too loudly; I can hardly hear her now. God! I hope she didn't…. She used to amuse herself with the thought of slipping grains of arsenic into his tea on mornings, and say that she would then live in peace, happiness and relative comfort for the rest of her days. Then with a sheepish grin she would add, "unless, that is, one of you were to then bump me off!"

"There has been a real tragedy." Her voice is strained, she is about to cry – I still recognize that trembling of her teeth. Yes, I am pretty sure it's about my father.

"Mummy, hold on a second. Just give me a second." I put down the phone on the floor and hold my chest. I take deep, slow breaths. I mustn't take too much time; it's a long distance call, thirty bucks a minute from her end. The thumping in my temples, too close to my ears, subsides only a shade. I pick up the phone and it increases again. "Mummy? I just had to catch my breath."

"No! No. It's okay. It's not about any of us. Not our family." Not our family. The blood in my temples begins to circulate a little easier and now that I have begun to relax I can feel just how seized-up my neck and jaw had become. My mind runs around again, but this time less frantically, out of curiosity, not terror. What the heck could it be that causes her to be up and calling at four in the morning? Another national revolution? (in a country so small as back there, everything that happens, happens in one's back yard; she takes national revolutions to heart) ... arson? (someone she knows has had their home or business burned to the ground? – who knows when it will be our turn?) ... one more family has been murdered, brutally wiped out (could have been ours, you know; that one-inch sheet of wood masquerading as a back door is a present to a thief) in yet another violent robbery...? a mass cult suicide involving children of one of her friends? (could have been one of her own) ... my ninety-something-year-old aunt...? but that wouldn't be tragic, that has been expected for quite a while. After the immense contracting and expanding of my temples and the relief that it's not about our family, any of the above would be anticlimactic.

"I couldn't sleep. I am in the kitchen drinking tea. Everyone else is asleep but I can't sleep. I can't stop thinking about it."

"Uh-huh." I don't want to interrupt her.

"Do you remember Donald and Douglas? Liz Baldeo's children?" I feel as if I am being suspended.

"Uh-huh, from next door, right? The twins?"

"Uh-huh. You probably don't remember them. They were only a couple of months old when you left."

"No, no. I do remember them. At least I remember when they were born. I guess that would make them about eight years old now, huh? What happened?"

"Well, Douglas died last night."

"Oh no!" I was so much expecting bad news about a member of my own family that relief makes my response sound trite to my own ears. I conscientiously soften my voice. "How come? What happened?" My mother ignores my question for the moment. I must just wait and let her tell me the way she wants it to unfold.

"Well, Liz and Harry are a mess. I can't sleep ... every few minutes I hear her wailing from next door. You know they tried to sedate her but the sedatives won't work. I looked outside just now and Harry is just standing in the dark out by the pomme-cythère tree in the back yard, with his hands over his face. And there isn't a thing anybody could do, really."

The reality of the neighbours, whom I have known since high school days, losing their son is creeping over me. "Oh-oh! I'm sorry to hear this. How did he die, Mummy?"

"Well, this is the thing. It's so tragic." She pauses, and in the long distance silence I can hear her sympathy and contemplation. "You know, the two boys always liked magic and all that sort of thing. They were always pretending to be in a circus, and doing tricks. You know, one day your father looked out and saw them walking along the ridge of the roof of their house, balancing themselves with broomsticks!"

"Goodness! Huh! But that is rather dangerous!"

"Well, last week Franklin Family Circus... " (the walls of my stomach weaken with the mention of the word *circus* and all the possibility of misadventure it instantly conjures up) "was here and since then the two boys have been putting on magic shows in the back yard for the other children in the neighbourhood. They saw an act at the circus that they decided to try out. Well, yesterday in front of a few other children from the neighbourhood – Paul Joselyn and Sara Beharry and some others you wouldn't know, about six of them altogether – Donald tied Douglas to the pommecythère tree, blindfolded himself and ... God! I can't believe it ... he started pelting knives ... I suppose to hit the tree right above Douglas's head."

"Oh my God!" I am left with hardly enough air in me to let the words out beyond a whisper. "Oh God, how awful!"

"No! No, no. That is not how he died. The knife did hit the tree above Douglas's head. It didn't touch him at all, but it shook up one big snake, long like a skipping rope but a little thicker, that was in a hole in the tree, and the thing darted down onto Douglas's shoulder and bit him on his neck right by his jugular."

"Oh noooo! How horrible!"

"Well, I was in my bedroom taking a nap and I heard the children screaming, so I jumped up to see what was going on and I could see Douglas tied to the tree, and the snake sliding down his chest. I wanted to die. Can you imagine?"

"Yes, I can." Too well. My eyes are closed, scrunched up tight against the image. Now I feel totally for Douglas, the terror he must have felt having a snake on his shoulder while his hands were tightly tied. "Was anyone at their house?"

"His mother was there and the yard boy who was working down in the front of the house. When they heard the screaming they rushed out too and the yard boy eventually killed the snake. But, you see, Douglas was tied up to the tree. They couldn't even get him untied without first killing the snake." She pauses and I remain silent, unable to respond. She adds, "Douglas died before they could get him to the hospital."

"Oh Mummy, that is awful. How is Donald? He must be in shock."

"He is. He is blaming himself. He just went crazy when they told him that Douglas had died. He started crazy-running into the wall, slamming his shoulder and his head into the brick, and they had to hold him down and sedate him too. Poor thing. That will stay with him forever. His only sibling! You know, the other day I saw that snake sunning on the concrete by the water tank at the back. Your father went to get the cutlass to kill it but when he came back it was gone. We were so worried, not knowing where it had gone to. This could have been any one of your sisters' or your brother's children, you know!"

With that sentence I notice my sympathy for Douglas and his family again curve into relief that her call was not about one of my own family members. Not to disrespect the gravity of my mother's empathy, I decide to indulge her and to hold on to the moment a bit longer by asking about Donald's and Douglas's grandmother. I remember her rocking on their balcony in the shade of large fern baskets on hot still afternoons. But my mother's voice expresses irritation with me.

"Their grandmother? You mean Harry's mother? But what is wrong with you, Sonita? What do you mean? She passed away about seven years ago. You know that. I phoned and told you. I distinctly remember, because it was on the very same day that my mother had passed away, twenty-eight years earlier."

She is indignant. Hurt. She has often said that this country has made me cold and uncaring about the people back home.

"Of course, Mummy. I'm sorry. It's hard to remember from up here." A sloppy, thoughtless mistake. It brings an uncomfortably ragged end to the call and to whatever it is that she had hoped I might provide for her.

I sit in the dark living room thinking of my mother sitting in her kitchen alone. It is now two-thirty; that was an expensive phone call. I think of the Baldeos: Liz and Harry and Donald, and Douglas. I have no idea what Douglas and Donald might have looked like now, but I do remember the twin pram with the two of them in it so many years ago. Soon I might forget that Douglas has passed away and, damn me, might even ask my mother how he is. She has made it her job to keep me informed of the deaths (even of people I have no memory of), but not taking part myself in their burials, I forget who has passed away and who was on the verge of doing so but recovered. Even though I am informed of each and every passing, I occasionally stupidly ask after them, and I do expect to see them when next I visit. I must make an effort to remember that Douglas has died.

It is difficult to return to sleep. I have dreaded such a middle-of-the-night call – much like this one, but about the passing of my own mother – for so very long that if I can be allowed to scrutinize the minutest details of my mind I will have to admit to a perverse disappointment that it was not at least about someone in my immediate family. I am instantly aware that the possibility of such a call still exists, and my frightened anticipation resumes right here in the dark.

It occurs to me now (and I must inscribe this in my head to relieve at least one level of panic) that there was no need to have raced for the phone when it rang. It couldn't have been ringing quite as long as it seemed; it's set to be received by the answering system on the fourth ring, and it was still ringing when I reached it.

The Upside-downness of the World as it Unfolds

I.

I was just about to type the word with which I would launch into my story, but that word has a way of evoking a memory of the attack of a slender 18" × 1½" length of wood sprung thwaa-aack! against a thinly-covered row of bones, and my knuckles remember the ache as if the pronouncement had come down only seconds ago, decommissioning my fingers. A simple, over-used word. Not one, however, that is overused in my back-home, but overused here, in this country of englishes (but not so many English folk as they themselves might like). The first time I used that word was some twenty-five years ago, in front of Mrs. Dora Ramsey, the ancient retired British tutor my parents hired to push, no, shove us through the common entrance exam. And ever since that usage, so many years back, I have had trouble even thinking the word.

Tdrrrrrring! a little bell rings, taking us back into the past. There it is again: tdrrrrrring! A glass of cow's milk and a plate of currant rolls ("dead fly cemetery," they are called, flaky pastry tri-angles studded with hundreds of dark reddish brown shrivelled currants) and the unpeeled cheeks of ripe julie mangoes sit on a kitchen table. Two girls, my sister Sharda and I, nine and ten years old, ignore the dead fly cemetery and grab the mangoes first, each cheek held up to the mouth, teeth sunk into the golden flesh, yellow creamy juice slipping down the corner of a mouth and running in a crooked egg-yellow rivulet down the finger, down the palm, down the arm to drip off the elbow. Sweet satisfaction and then the two girls grow sullen, sticky yellow elbows digging defiantly into the table, as they prop their chins into their sweet-smelling palms. Their mother snaps, "Stop lahayin and drink up that milk. If you weren't such dodo-heads you wouldn't have to go to private lessons. And you have no choice. Take that sulk off your face this minute!"

"But Mummy...."

"Don't but with me. You are going if I have to drag you there myself!"

She didn't drag us there herself, Boyie the chauffeur did. He drove us (our reluctance made the car sluggish) three blocks and around the corner to a house set far back in a cul-de-sac where, without our having to announce ourselves, the tall wrought-iron gates rumbled and parted at their centre seam. Boyie never crossed the gate; he was afraid that it would close behind him, trapping him, subjecting him to synonyms, antonyms, onomatopoeia and other words he heard us hurling at each other as if they were ultimate insults.

"You synonym!"

"Do you want to get subjunctived?"

"Onomatopoeia sme-ell, onomatopoeia sme-ell."

"No they don't. You do. You smell."

So Sharda and I walked from the bottom of the driveway, with our exercise books, vocabulary and usage texts, and finely sharpened yellow pencils, up a long and winding asphalt path, whispering encouragement to each other through motionless lips. We looked hard through the jacaranda and bougainvillaea shrubs scattered missionary-style all over the lawn, trying to spot the

clammy cold white English hand and lordly eyes of the con-
troller of the gates groaning shut behind us.

We always entered the house through the kitchen. Widowed
Mrs. Ramsey, living out her days and thawing out her marrow in
the colonies, would stand at the top stair waiting by the back
door, watching us mount each step as if we were carrying sacks
of mangoes on our backs. She would make us wipe our shoes on
the husk mat at the top stair outside the kitchen and push us
through the kitchen where Rommel, the Rhodesian Ridgeback,
lay on the cool terrazzo with his hind legs sprawled straight out
behind him, guarding his pot of rice, bones and leftovers melting
down under a bubbling froth to dog-food mush on the stove-top.

Following Mrs. Ramsey's spreading frame, we meandered
through the house of curios commemorating the coronation of
Queen Elizabeth in 1952. We slid our hands along our upside-
down reflections, clear like a still lake's, on the 200-year-old
colonial-style mahogany dining table and chairs, to the verandah
with purple, yellow and white hanging orchids, potted pink
anthuriums, and a wall of purple bougainvillaea. Shading the
patio was an S-shaped avocado tree, with S-shaped branches
weighed down low by ripe avocadoes hanging like Mrs. Ramsey's
heavy breasts (which Sharda and I were always trying to see
more of, to know what secrets their Britishness held), and as big,
the length from an elbow to one's outstretched middle finger.
Nothing in Mrs. Ramsey's garden was mongrel, everything was
trophy- and certificate-winning, deeper in colour, bigger, contorted or striped or variegated hybrids; everything was straightened and tied with plant wire and trained with trellises. On the
edge of all of this, in the cool evening breeze, is where we sat and
were taught to behave like the well-brought-up young ladies in
her back-home where she had once long, long ago been the prin-

cipal of a private high school for girls only.

New words were fitted in our mouths and we were taught how to use them. Word: pagan (pā' gən), *n.* 1. one who is not a Christian, Moslem, or Jew; heathen. 2. one who has no religion. 3. a non-Christian. Sentence: The pagans of Indian ancestry pray to images of a dancing Shiva, a blue Krishna, or the cow.

Top marks.

We recited multiplication tables from the back cover of our exercise book, and often when time permitted we were given a complimentary lesson in flower arrangement or table etiquette. How, with knife and fork, to eat roti and curried châtaigne, which her Afro-Indo-Trinidadian half-day maid cooked. Soup and cereal, to tip or not to tip, when and how. And how to eat a mango correctly. Never ripping with hands and teeth, or slurping off the edge of a cheek; always cutting with a knife and fork. Slice off cheeks, grid the inside with knife, then slide knife under the sections and release with fork.

One night Mrs. Ramsey tried to slice up and grid my family. My parents, my sister and I were invited for supper; Mrs. Ramsey served plump, perfumed and runny mangoes for dessert. My parents ate their cheeks the way mangoes have always been enjoyed in Trinidad, cupped in one hand and sucked and slurped, the meat dragged off the skin with happy grinning teeth. Mrs. Ramsey sat straight-backed as she gridded her mango cheeks and proceeded with knife and fork to deal with one manageable square at a time. Without a word to each other, Sharda and I weighed the wisdom of choosing one mango-eating method over the other and decided to decline dessert.

That night when our Ahji, Daddy's mother, came to put us to bed with her childhood textbook of the Hindi alphabet and wanted us to learn her mother's language, we both said that we didn't care about India and didn't want to learn a language that only old and backward people spoke. That night Ahji gasped and died a little.

Oh! The word I began this preamble with, or rather without (you see, this is still the preamble, not yet the story!) ... Well, days later, again in the cul-de-sac, I answered some command or other with the word – are you ready for it? – with the word *okay*, and Sharda and I watched Mrs. Ramsey catch a fit, hopping and squealing.

"I beg your pardon! Did I hear correctly? What was that you answered me with?"

And I meekly repeated my word, thinking it inoffensive and not warranting comment: *okay*. She again hopped, scowled and made her eyes beady tight, and brought out Rudyard, the wooden ruler. She let me have it over my knuckles until I felt a hot wet ooze slipping out from between my knotted legs, and then she explained through clenched teeth, "*Okay* is slang. Abbreviation of *oll korrect* – itself a re-spelling [read mis-spelling] of *all correct*. Slang. Do you understand *slang*? Look it up!"

I fumbled through my dog-eared navy blue pocket dictionary and was too confused to read full phrases but several words leapt out from under the heading *slang* and left an indelible impression: ... *nonstandard ... subculture ... arbitrary ... ephemeral coinages ... spontaneity ... peculiar ... raciness.*

And then she squealed, "*Okay* is not simply slang; above all it is an Americanism, that history-less upstart, a further butchering of our Oxford! Never, [pause for emphasis, and close-up on mouth pursed anus-tight] never let me hear that ... that ... that meaningless utterance again!"

On that evening I did not simply learn about slang; a revelation occurred to me, a shift as vivid as when one's sinuses suddenly quake and move around behind one's face as the passages clear. I realized that White (I assumed that America was White [from TV and *Time Magazine*] and I assumed that England was also White [from my first history book, and the second, and the third; from *Coronation Street*, *The Avengers*, *Women's Weekly*]) ... I realized that White is not all the same. Mrs. Ramsey's upturned chin and haughty reserve appealed to my parents, whose propensity to supplicate was well served, but the American families who were in Trinidad to govern our oil fields were viewed as Whites who had gone to seed. They flaunted their lack of gentility with their leisurely patio barbecues (imagine serving guests on paper plates and with plastic utensils!) and pot lucks (imagine a hostess expecting her guests to bring their own food!). It went unchallenged for me that in the hierarchy of Whites, British was Queen and American was peasant.

Early in life I already displayed the trait of championing the underdog, and so much better if the underdog were also "Other." India was not "Other" enough for me. India was at home in Trinidad. Ahji did not bring out her alphabet book again but she quietly, subversively and obstinately brought India into our house by intensifying her wearing of saris, singing of bhajans, and performing of conspicuous evening poojas by herself. The house filled up every evening with smoke from camphor squares and the radio no longer played calypsos or the American Top 40, only music from Indian films and Hindu religious music. North America became the "Other" underdog for me. When it came time for me to go abroad for further education, this is where I ended up, to the veritable irritation of my parents.

Tdrrrrrring! Tdrrrrrring! And we (you and I, not the cast of the preamble; you and I have left them all behind now) find ourselves feeling cold, hugging our shoulders, and bouncing from foot to foot, even though we are indoors. Tdrrrrrring! and we look outside and see tall buildings, low grey sky, a couple of scraggly pine trees, and some exhaust-greyed flowerless shrubs here and there. We have arrived in North America, Canada to be precise, downtown Vancouver to be razor sharp. And the word *okay* is no longer italicized, even though there is a faint ringing in my knuckles still.

2.

Okay! So now that I want to know about India, Ahji has died, and I can't afford to go there. And White friends, unlike my White childhood tutor, no longer want to whiten me but rather they want to be brown and sugary like me, so much so that two of them in particular have embarked on a mission to rub back in the brown that Mrs. Ramsey tried so hard to bleach out. It was my taste for "Other" music (now that I live in North America "Otherness" is elsewhere) that bumped me into those two, whose interest was in "Other" cultures.

Ever since I saw Zahara, my ex-sweetie, walking hand-in-hand with another woman, I have been crying to the music of love-sick Sudanese musicians. Of course I debated questions of exoticization and exploitation by the World Beat craze, but always I assuaged my conscience with the thought that Zahara is Muslim and from Zaire, close enough to Sudan, and since I had bedded with her I had some right to this music as a balm for my sick heart. I was misguided perhaps, but those who are losers in love usually are.

Ever since she had left me I found myself lured daily to the music store that specializes in World Beat music. With a good dose of contempt curling a sneer in my upper lip, I would, nevertheless, buy up every piece of mournful beseeching coming out of Muslim Africa. When my mother found out (a story in itself) that I preferred the company of women, she said that I had put a knife in her heart, but when she heard that the object of this preference was Muslim, she said that I had shoved the knife deeper and twisted it in her Hindu heart. I hope that she does not have the opportunity to see, let alone hear, my CD collection: Nusrat, Hamza, Abdel Aziz, Abdel Gadir, etc.

The blond, stringy-haired man at the counter was trying to get me interested in a CD by Mohamed Gubara from Sudan. With my eyes closed, I leaned against the glass case which displayed harmonicas and guitar strings, and listened to the Sudanese musician bleating tabanca songs and strumming the tambour.

I imagined his face, his eyes shut also, and his tambour caressed at his chest like a lover he was embracing and singing to. The chimes above the doorway to the store tinkled under Mohamed Gubara's voice and a hint of men's cologne underneath the flowery scent of a woman announced a presence more arresting than Mohamed Gubara's music. I opened my eyes and recognized the shortness of the hair, the breastlessness of shirt, the Birkenstocks and grey socks. I thought that she recognized similar things in my appearance, but I learned later that she had had no idea that I might be "family." The reason she stared and smiled and then came over to talk was that she frequently visited India. Meet Meghan.

— Did I want to go for a cup of chai next door?

— I don't drink tea.

— A glass of lassi, perhaps?

— I'd prefer a cappuccino.

And so over cappuccinos and an attraction to her, I wiggled my way into hinting of my sexual persuasion, which I had correctly assumed was the same as hers. We exchanged phone numbers and for the next forty-eight hours I leapt to answer every phone call, hoping that it would be her. Her call came after seventy-two hours.

— Did I remember her?

— Uh, yes, how was she enjoying her new CDs?

— Oh, they're just wonderful. How about dinner? At an Indian restaurant that she frequents?

— Uh, sure, okay. Why not. (Yes! Yes! Yes! Even though a too-long absence from home has created in me an intense intolerance of Indian food.)

All but wrapped and tied up with a bow (I cut my own blend of men's and women's scent, blow-dried my hair twice – the first time I was a little too intense and one side was bouffant-ish and the other not), I arrived at the restaurant to find that she and another woman were seated waiting for me. Enter Virginia, her partner for the last five years, of whom she had not hinted before.

No need to have made my bed and washed the dishes.

3.

Meghan and Virginia turned out to be peace-seekers to a fault. Quietly, with no heroism whatsoever, they retreated from everything remotely resembling indulgence. Their desire for peace, harmony and one big happy world was not, to my relief, accompanied by incense-burning and patchouli fragrances! Nor had they fallen into the crystal craze. And one other thing: they had a good-natured contempt for tissue-thin Indian skirts with little claustrophobia-inducing mango-seed paisleys and hemlines with frayed tassels. Thank the powers that be! They picked a safe, simple lifestyle.

They had, however, made one big-time purchase: a hot-off-the-press pristine four-door Mazda 626. It was a little expensive, but undeniably a sensible buy – not what one could call excessive (not one of those limited edition types). After all, who expects reliability and safety to come without a price tag attached?

In all the time that I have known them I have never once heard either one raise her voice, in vexation or in jubilation. So I can't really say that I minded when they spoke about Peace and Oneness with an accent or in the sing-song tone of the fumbling-bumbling Indian stereotype in Peter Sellers's movies. They didn't mean to mock or be malicious. Take my word for it. In fact, they were both genuine in their desire to be Indian. Meghan could slide her neck horizontally from shoulder to shoulder like the small vibrantly coloured papier-mâché Indian dancer that used to sit on our windowsill, around the corner and down the street from Mrs. Ramsey's, its head dangling sideways in the wind. (To my shame, to this day I am still unable to slide my neck, or give a convincing imitation of an Indian accent.) Sliding her neck, Meghan would say in an accent thick and syrupy as a jilebi, "All we want is peace and happiness in this world. I am wishing you these this very morning!"

Around her neck she wore a little pendant, a brass globe the size of a "jacks" ball, with the world in bas relief on it, hanging from a shiny black satin cord. A sadhu she bumped into in Bangalore, years ago, had given it to her. After giving her blessings, she would grasp the world and give it a little shake. The world would tinkle brilliantly, the sound slowly fading as if it were moving outward into some other consciousness. Tdrrrrrring! And again, Tdrrrrrring!

Meghan and Virginia had been to India travelling around several times, separately, before they knew each other. In fact, that is where they met; Meghan was heading south from Calcutta to Madras, ashram-hopping, and Virginia was making the opposite trip, from Mysore in the south to Varanasi up north. They met on a hustle-and-bustle street somewhere in between, intuitively yanked together like magnets: two White Canadian women searching, searching, for what they did not quite know, until, that is, they found each other. Destiny. Mission. Karma. They realized that they both had Ukrainian roots (they have since found out that they are distantly related), another magnet for them. They quickly discovered that they had much more than that in common, too. On the day that they met, Meghan did a string of pirouettes, one after the other, until she faced north, and she headed in that direction, accompanying Virginia. But that is a story in itself, and they can tell their own story. I am tired of telling other people's romantic stories.

At some point they came back home to Canada, and a couple of months later left the hustle, bustle and overall coldness of Toronto to head for Vancouver, which is a lot closer to India. They say that when they go down to English Bay and dip their toes in the water they can feel a current of seductive tassa drumming vibrating all the way from the heart of India, encircling their feet and rising up in them. Sometimes lying in bed at night in their North Van home, nestled in the quiet, forested uplands, they hear chanting from the ashram in Calcutta.

It is from them that I learned about Varanasi, the river Ganga and Calcutta in such grassroots earthy detail that I can smell and feel particles of dusty heat collecting in my nostrils. They can decode my ancestors' ceremonies for me, when what I know of them is mostly from the colourful coffee-table picture books that are always on sale at the Book Warehouse for $4.95.

The first time I met them I heard Meghan say "acha" at some point in our conversation, and I let it go, thinking it was a Ukrainian expression. Later, when she said "chalo" and then "nahi," I had to cock my head sideways and ask if those were the same Hindi words I had heard Ahji use. They came naturally to Meghan. She often exclaimed in longer Hindi sentences, catching me off guard, making me feel ignorant and like a charlatan. Ahji would have been baffled by the upside-downness of the world as it unfolds.

The only Indian words I know are those on the menus in Indian restaurants and in my very own *Indian Cookery by Mrs. Balbir Singh*. From the first day when I arrived in Canada people would say, "Oh, great! You can teach me to cook Indian food, and that tea, what is it called? Masala tea? Chai? You know, the one with the spices." But I didn't know, hadn't heard of such a tea until I came up here. Instead of disappointing people before I even got a chance to make any friends, I went out and bought that cookbook, which has just about saved my face more than a few times. Mrs. Singh taught me words like vindaloo, mulligatawny, bhuna, matar, pullao and gosht, and of course, roti in some of its varieties: chapati, puri, naan, and so on.

It was inevitable that Meghan and Virginia would one day invite me to go with them to the Hare Krishna temple out in Ferrinbridge. "Come learn a little about your culture!" they suggested in the jovial manner of those enlightened to such absurdities of life. Feeling like a cultural orphan, I decided to go. I was only a little surprised to find out that they were Krishna followers. You see, it is not that I was surprised that two White women would belong to that movement. In fact, I was always under the impression that Hare Krishnas were, indeed, White, having been introduced to the movement by the Beatles, and then having seen with my own eyes only White folk chanting the names of Hindu gods and beating Indian tassa drums at airports in Miami, New York and London. It is only recently, at the Peace March downtown, that I've seen among the Krishna contingency a handful – well, less than that, really – of Browns awkwardly partaking in the clapping, swaying, chanting, drumming and tinkling amidst a sea of White men wearing orange kurtas and white dotis, and White women wearing thin heaven-white cotton saris, the women so emaciated and long-limbed that their saris, which were tightly wrapped instead of draped, looked like some type of garment other than a sari (perhaps a mummy's outer encasement, with an ohrni thrown over the head). It made me wonder who came first, the White followers or the Indian ones. Who converted whom.

What surprised me was that these two women, who were a lot closer to my living room than the Beatles or fleeting orange kurtas and nameless chanting faces in airports, these acquaintances of mine were Krishna followers. These two very ordinary, well-heeled (suede Birks) and responsible people! Well, what I really mean to say is "these good-looking White dykes!"

I readily decided to swallow my shame that these two were better Indians than I, and to go ingest some of the sounds, smells, colours and tastes (everyone talks of the free vegetarian meal after a prayer meeting) of my foreparents' homeland.

Sunday evening, the evening I was to learn a little about my culture, the pristine Mazda 626 sidled up to the curb in front of my apartment building. The inside of the car was ablaze with colour: Virginia's grinning face peeped out from under the cherdo of a brilliant red silk sari, her face framed by a navy blue border with discriminating flecks of silver paisleys. Meghan's cherdo hung around her neck, leaving her sandy-coloured head hovering in that dangerous place where one cannot pin her down to being female or male. Boyish one minute, unmistakably woman the next. And then boyish again.

Meghan was immensely pleased with herself. Her silk sari was forest green, with tiny gold paisleys all over and a thick, heavily-embroidered border of silver and gold. My own plain white T-shirt, dark blue rayon slacks, Dr. Martens' brogues and white socks (I guessed, correctly, that we would have to remove our shoes, so I wore a pair of brand-new dressy socks that I had been saving for a special occasion) made me feel like a party-pooper going to a costume party. "Wow! You guys look great!" and other exclamations came out of my mouth, but the thoughts in my head flipped back and forth between "God, do I ever feel under-dressed, shabby, shown-up as a cultural ignoramus" and "What the heck do you want with dressing up in saris and praying to Indian gods? What business do you have showing me what I have lost? Go check out your own ancestry!" A string of unprintable thoughts and expletives surprised me. Would have turned Mrs. Ramsey blue.

Meghan pulled the car away from the curb and Virginia turned back to talk to me. When I saw her blue satin blouse I realized that I had unconsciously harboured the thought that they would be wearing T-shirts instead of sari blouses. After a few minutes I became aware that I had overdone the "Gosh! They're sooo beautiful" sentiments, and I felt quite awkward. When we got out of the car I saw their full saris, faultlessly wrapped. The pleats of the patli were equally spaced, perfectly placed. I was in the mood to bet that they had had the patli arranged and then permanently sewn in place.

I was not the only South Asian at the ashram, as I had expected to be. In fact, a good half of the modest gathering was Brown-skinned. None of the Brown men wore the orange and white of the Krishnas, though. They wore quiet, polite Western suits. The Brown women all wore modest day saris. Dressed as I was, the only female Browny in Western wear, I understood, as if it were a revelation, Ahji's panic and distress at the unravelling of her culture right before her eyes.

Virginia and Meghan, with eyes closed, clapped and swayed to the chaotic drumming and the tuneless chanting of the all-White leaders. I stood as stiffly as an old piece of dried toast, with my hands clasped behind my back. The other Brown folk, on the periphery of the room, not at all central to the goings-on, clapped discreetly, without their bodies exhibiting their spiritual jubilance.

In a temple of Krishna and Rama, surrounded by murals depicting scenes from the Bhagavad Gita, among peace-desiring people full of benevolence, my temperature – temper, actually – rose. The sermon on a particular chapter of the Gita was delivered by His Holiness, a White man in orange, with a head shaved except for a thin tail of hair emanating from the upper back of his head. He sat on a throne surrounded by his entourage of White devotees. He had just returned from India full of inspiration and energy and was passing out stories of the work being done there to complete the building of a city and centre of Krishna devotion. "Go to India," he said repeatedly, grinning impishly with the privilege of having done so himself several times.

The men sat closest to him, in front, and the women sat at the back. The Brown women fell into their places at the very back, against the wall. Midway through the sermon a young man came to fetch women, who were needed in the kitchen to serve the food. He crossed over and meandered among the congregation of White women who were nearest to him, heading for the Brown ones. They dutifully rose and followed him into the kitchen, missing the ending of the sermon.

I wondered what wisdom it was (if that is what it was) that kept people from committing crimes right there and then. A familiar burning touched my knuckles, but this time it was from too tight a fist wanting to impact with history. An urgent rage buzzed around my head and ears like a swarm of crazed mosquitoes. I unfisted my hands and flayed them around my head, brushing away the swarming past and present.

I looked over at my two friends sitting at my side. Meghan and Virginia, genuine in their desire to find that point where all division ceases and we unite as one, shone radiantly. Meghan followed my eyes as I watched the Brown women walking single-file to the kitchen. In her favourite accent, full of empathy, she said, "Pretty sexist, eh! That's a problem for us too."

Tdrrrrring! Oh! there's my doorbell!

A letter from back home, from my mother. In the unfamiliar tone of her written English she writes, " ... She gave me her prized potted scorpion orchid just days before she passed away. As if she had a premonition! She had asked your Papa, quite some time back, to be the executor of her will. Her wish was that he contact her step-son, George Arthur Ramsey, in Surrey, England and have her body flown back to him for burial among their kin. We did our best for our good friend, to whom Sharda and you owe thanks for your skills in the English language. After several telegrams back and forth, Papa found George living in Philadelphia, U.S.A. with his new bride, an Indian woman from East Africa. [I automatically wonder if she is Muslim.] So her body was sent to him there, where he held a funeral for her. We sincerely hope that this arrangement was okay.... "

SHANI MOOTOO is an Indo-Trinidadian-Canadian writer who lives in Vancouver. She is also a visual artist and video-maker. Her visual art has been exhibited in many solo and group shows, including "Memory and Desire: the Voices of Eleven Women of Culture" at the Vancouver Art Gallery in 1992. In the past two years she has written and directed four videos, including "English Lesson" (1991) and "Wild Woman in the Woods" (1993), which have shown in festivals locally and internationally. Her writing has been featured in several *Gallerie Women Artists' Monographs,* in *Fuse* magazine and in *The Skin on Our Tongues. Out on Main Street* is her first book of short fiction.

KAUSAR NIGITA is a visual artist and print-maker who was born in Pakistan and now lives in Vancouver. She studied etching at Les Ateliers des Beaux-Arts in Paris and lithography at Print Workshop in Sydney, Australia. She says of her work: "My Indo-Persian roots are apparent in my style, which is sometimes ornate, sometimes calligraphic, sometimes both." Her recent exhibits include the solo show "River of Dreams" at the Vancouver East Cultural Centre Gallery (1992) and "Rituelles" at Alliance Française, Ottawa.

PRESS GANG PUBLISHERS FEMINIST CO-OPERATIVE is committed to producing quality books with social and literary merit. We prioritize Canadian women's work and include writing by lesbians and by women from diverse cultural and class backgrounds. Our list features vital and provocative fiction, poetry and non-fiction.

A free catalogue is available from Press Gang Publishers, 603 Powell Street, Vancouver, B.C. V6A 1H2 Canada